Welcome to…

The Hollywood Hills Clinic

*Where doctors to the stars work miracles by day—
and explore their hearts' desires by night…*

When hotshot doc James Rothsberg started the clinic
six years ago he dreamed of a world-class facility, catering
to Hollywood's biggest celebrities, and his team are
unrivalled in their fields. Now, as the glare of the media
spotlight grows, the Hollywood Hills Clinic is teaming up
with the pro-bono Bright Hope Clinic, and James is reunited
with Dr Mila Brightman…the woman he jilted at the altar!

When it comes to juggling the care of Hollywood A-listers
with care for the underprivileged kids of LA *anything* can
happen…and sizzling passions run high in the shadow of
the red carpet. With everything at stake for James, Mila
and the Hollywood Hills Clinic medical team
their biggest challenges have only just begun!

The Hollywood Hills Clinic miniseries:

Dear Reader,

Liam and Grace are the first characters I've written about who haven't come from the void of my own subconscious. They came to me as part of a massive outline the editors unleashed on a gaggle of us writers to give life to. So I didn't make them, but I do believe I made them into the twisted little monkeys I do so love writing about.

I dearly love an 'older brother's best friend' storyline, and all the angst that comes along with it. But I also got to run with another favourite combo of mine: girl-next-door and super-unattainable and damaged hero. Or, as it actually is here, girl-next-door and junior high crush becomes high school first love, becomes subject of the most humiliating night of her life, becomes the celebrity crush whose image she can't avoid, becomes… You get the picture.

Hope you enjoy the ride—and if you like the glimpses of secondary characters who've made it into these pages check out their books in The Hollywood Hills Clinic series!

Amalie Xo

AmalieBerlin.com/Contact.html

Facebook.com/Amalie.Berlin

Twitter: @AmalieBerlin

TAMING HOLLYWOOD'S ULTIMATE PLAYBOY

BY
AMALIE BERLIN

Published in Great Britain 2016
By Mills & Boon, an imprint of HarperCollins*Publishers*
1 London Bridge Street, London, SE1 9GF

© 2016 Harlequin Books S.A.

*Special thanks and acknowledgement are given to Amalie Berlin
for her contribution to* The Hollywood Hills Clinic *series*

ISBN: 978-0-263-06491-9

Printed and bound in Great Britain
by CPI Antony Rowe, Chippenham, Wiltshire

Amalie Berlin lives with her family and critters in Southern Ohio, and writes quirky and independent characters for Mills & Boon Medical Romance. She likes to buck expectations with unusual settings and situations, and believes humour can be used powerfully to illuminate truth—especially when juxtaposed against intense emotions. Love is stronger and more satisfying when your partner can make you laugh through times when you don't have the luxury of tears.

Books by Amalie Berlin

Mills & Boon Medical Romance

New York City Docs

Surgeons, Rivals...Lovers

Craving Her Rough Diamond Doc
Uncovering Her Secrets
Return of Dr Irresistible
Breaking Her No-Dating Rule
Falling for Her Reluctant Sheikh

Visit the Author Profile page
at millsandboon.co.uk for more titles.

To the awesome and lovely writers who populate the
#1k1hr hashtag on Twitter. Without you this book
would've never been done by deadline.

And to the other awesome and lovely writers at the
Harlequin Writers' Circle forums. Without you guys I
maybe wouldn't have needed Twitter to make deadline.
But I've never had so much fun or felt so helpful and
productive while procrastinating

Xo

Praise for
Amalie Berlin

'*Falling for Her Reluctant Sheikh* by author Amalie
Berlin blew my mind away! This story is definitely worth
re-reading and fans are in for a medical treat!'

—*Goodreads*

'Amalie Berlin has proved she's one of the best medical
authors of today and her stories will for ever have a place
on my reading shelf.'

—*Contemporary Romance Reviews* on
Return of Dr Irresistible

'A sexy, sensual, romantic, heartwarming and purely
emotional, romantic, bliss-filled read. I very much look
forward to this author's next book and being transported
to a world of pure romance brilliance!'

—*Goodreads* on
Craving Her Rough Diamond Doc

CHAPTER ONE

"Now for the hard part…" Liam Carter muttered, hauling himself out of the deeply comfortable chair in James Rothsberg's office at The Hollywood Hills Clinic.

"The hard part?" James asked, politely rising in tandem with him.

Why had he said that? James didn't need to know how shaky his plan was.

"Walking," Liam said, offering an explanation he knew James would believe.

"I can get you a wheelchair and have you wheeled down to the treatment rooms…"

"No." He raised a hand, laughing a little. Limping and still upright, even with pain, trumped being wheeled around. "No, I can make it."

Liam hadn't seen Grace in six years, and he'd damned well make her re-acquaintance on his feet. No matter how much it hurt.

He tested his balance and found it before he found the appropriate expression to conceal the pain.

James rounded his desk, hand outstretched to shake. "Don't be surprised if Grace insists on crutches."

Even without his desire to save face with Grace, if anyone saw him in a wheelchair or on crutches, word would travel, and the people he spent ninety-five percent of his life making happy would begin to question his suitability for the project.

Liam mustered a smile and shook the offered hand, then turned toward the door. "I'm sure we'll work something out. Grace always was good at creative problem solving." In their amicable past, the one that had ended for them that one night. The one he'd never have James know about, the land where nothing ever suddenly exploded. One terrible…and amazing night.

There had been plenty of great years before hormones had become involved, but the punctuation on that sentence assured their first meeting in years would be anything but normal.

For someone who lied for a living, doing so off script always left a bad taste in his mouth, so he left it at that. It had to be Grace…

Minimizing his limp as much as possible, Liam exited the office and made his way to the elevator he'd been directed to. The Hollywood Hills Clinic lived up to its reputation of clean, modern elegance, not that he could really appreciate it right now.

Two days and the best splint money could buy hadn't even put a dent in the pain that radiated up his leg with every step. Liam would swear his ankle hurt more now than the day he'd sprained it. But despite the pain and the all-looming discomfort, the prospect of seeing Grace Watson again still had him moving a little faster.

How would the years have changed her? Would he find her still the slender, athletic girl she'd been, light on curves but with quiet, supple strength? Maybe he was nervous for no good reason, and time apart could've extinguished that youthful spark between them. It might not even come up.

Through Nick, he knew that Grace had worked in

professional sports, helping athletes keep fighting fit. She could help him. He just had to convince her. Pretend their last meeting had never happened. They were both fully adults now, and adults ignored unpleasant things all the time in order to keep things cordial.

A short ride down and he stepped off the elevator. The more he walked, the more the spark of anticipation grew in his gut, and the faster he hobbled.

He just had to pretend. Pretend the image of her in that flimsy black lingerie wasn't still etched crisply into his mind...six years later.

Hard to believe it had been that long.

By the time he'd reached the treatment rooms, the buzz on the back of his neck was enough to drown out the constant pain grinding through his ankle, or at least enough to distract him from it.

He stepped through the door of the treatment room, and before he'd even looked over the various equipment and exercise areas, he knew she wasn't there. It felt empty.

Back in the hallway, he could see double doors at the end marked for the therapy pool. If she was anywhere, she'd be there.

Pools were as common as palms in Southern California and, while growing up, anytime she'd had a few minutes to spare, she'd spent them in the Watson family's pool.

He approached the edge of the pool just in time to see her turn underwater and push off the side. He knew from the way she moved that it was Grace even through the shimmer of water. Sleek and fast, she powered through the water toward the far end.

Mermaid. He shook his head and felt himself smiling despite the nerves in the pit of his stomach. At least that hadn't changed.

Maybe their reunion would be exactly like those old times. Maybe she'd reach the edge of the water and pretend to want a hand out, only to jerk him in with her.

Another underwater turn and she swam far enough before surfacing to speak of impressive lung power, then cut a path through the water toward him, straight as an arrow despite an unmarked lane.

Taking advantage of the seconds it would take her to reach his end of the pool, Liam ambled back toward the doorway to give her some space to exit the water, and avoid the urge to play with her. This wasn't the old days, and he wasn't seventeen anymore.

He saw her hand reach for the edge of the pool and heard her rapid breathing. She'd seen him when her head had cleared the water while breathing, or she'd seen someone there with her.

Grace's head now popped over the edge and before he knew it she was emerging from the water, toned, tanned, and with the kind of curves that made the black bikini she wore look exactly like that lingerie…

No, not exactly. She hadn't really had much in the way of hips last time. Now even her curves had curves.

His breath caught as their eyes met, but as she swung a leg up onto the edge of the pool one arm buckled and she toppled back into the water with a splash.

"Grace?" Had she hit something when she'd fallen back in? The concrete edge could do some damage…

He hobbled forward again.

Through training and sheer effort, Grace managed not to suck down a lungful of chlorinated water as she went under.

Broad shoulders.

Dark hair.

Eyes crystal and blue, like the inside curl of a summer wave.

Liam Carter.

What the devil was Liam doing there?

She grasped the edge of the pool and kicked hard as she pulled herself up again, turning immediately to plop sideways on the tiles, as graceless as a walrus, and breathing about as hard as one in full flounder.

Through sheer luck, she managed not to smash her face into the floor.

A walrus in a bikini was bad enough, one with an injury would just make it so much worse. And the last time she'd seen him, she'd— *Oh, God.*

Suddenly, she was eighteen again, and full to bursting with humiliation. Not the years-old variety—the kind you felt and then discarded—it felt as fresh as newly picked daisies, and her inner walrus wanted nothing but to escape back to the water.

Before the blazing heat roasting her cheeks could spread to the rest of her visible flesh, Grace snatched up her towel and climbed to her feet, whisking it around her before she'd even truly found her balance.

This wasn't happening.

This was...*chlorine poisoning*. Had to be.

Or maybe oxygen deprivation.

She needed a mask.

Or just to get out of there. Before he figured out her transparent panic. Or saw the scars. Proof of yet more foolishness. And she'd really like him to think she'd come through that unmarked, or that they were basically invisible...since he'd never even deigned to visit her hospital room after it had happened. Not that she'd have wanted him to.

Liam had his hands up, a gesture of surrender, but his eyes reeked of concern—she'd assume it was fake except she'd seen that look before. Same frown. Same posture. Different setting...

But she was practically in the same freaking outfit. It was too much to hope this wasn't real. She never got that lucky.

"You're all right." He said the words more than asked. "I didn't mean to interrupt. I was just here... Thought I'd say hello."

As he spoke, he backpedaled from the room about as smoothly as her first attempt to get out of the pool, strongly favoring one leg.

She tucked the corner of the towel to form a tight band above her breasts and, once covered, looked down at his feet—not only to indulge her curiosity but to have something as far from his head as possible to examine kept accidental eye contact from recurring.

Which was when she noticed one ill-fitting shoe, the sides bulging out from a splint supporting his ankle.

She coughed to force words through her tight throat. "You're usually a better actor than that, aren't you?"

Thankfully she hadn't also honked when she'd spoken.

Grace shifted, arms crossing over her waist as if that would cover her better, or make sure he didn't start drawing the same parallels between this and the last time she'd set eyes on him.

Pretend this was normal. Pretend the thought of running away didn't make her feet tingle and her knees itch with anticipation. Say normal person words.

"Are you here to see me, Liam... Mr....Liam?" She

usually tried to be professional when addressing prospective patients, but "Mr. Carter" felt even weirder than "Liam." But all of this felt wrong. Bad-dream wrong. Naked-without-your-homework-on-the-day-of-the-big-exam wrong.

What did a woman call someone from her past she no longer had a relationship with but whom she'd once forced to see her in her underwear? What was the proper, professional comportment for that situation?

"Or someone else, maybe?" Please, God, a lightning bolt would be good right about now. She could use a little smiting. Maybe not enough to die. There were lessons to teach actors to cry on command, where could she get lessons to learn to faint on command? Shouldn't there be some holistic expert in pressure points who could teach her something for this kind of situation? Just in case it should come in handy again in the future.

"I was thinking…" He stopped the denial and shrugged his affirmation. "Yes. I'm here to see you." He stopped his limping backward cadence and his arms fell lifelessly at his sides. "I sprained it. And with my schedule right now…"

Treatment. This wasn't a coincidence. At least treatment meant she had something to do other than stand around and wonder if he could see her nipples through her bikini top as he'd been able to do through that ridiculous bra. Or the other stupid thoughts shouting in her mental echo chamber, none of which would make him go away any faster. But treatment might.

Examine him. Offer advice. Refer him to someone else. Call it a day!

Good plan.

But get dressed first.

Act normal. Like nothing is wrong.

"Can you make it back to the treatment room?" She glanced into his eyes long enough to see the furrow of irritation marring his too-handsome features and was almost proud she finally sounded normal and professional.

"Of course."

"Okay. I'll just dry off, change, and then come check on you. Have a seat in one of the reclining chairs and get your foot up. It'll help with the throbbing." More sane words.

He paused a moment and then nodded. Without another word, he pivoted on his good leg and hobbled back out into the hallway, leaving Grace to make a beeline for the locker room to change.

Had Nick sent him here? Her brother was still friends with Liam. They had a bond that never weakened, even through the months when Liam was too busy to hang out or whatever it was they did together. Grace didn't know. She always tried her best not to know what Liam was up to, as much as was humanly possible in LA when she couldn't even go to the store to buy toothpaste without seeing his pearly whites gracing the cover of some magazine.

WORLD'S SEXIEST MAN!
   How Does Sexy Megastar Liam Carter Keep Those Rock-Hard Abs?
   Hollywood's Most Wanted talks life, love, and his favorite blah-blah-blah...

Or the ones she'd seen that morning when buying fruit: racks of tabloid headlines about Liam destroying his ex-girlfriend, who could only find comfort in the pills she got hooked on.

With minimal toweling efforts, she dried just enough to get her clothes back on without sticking, roughly combed her hair back into a ponytail, and stuffed her feet into sandals.

She'd go and examine him. Figure out what he was doing and what he should be doing to get back on his feet as quickly as possible. Fetch some crutches, maybe a different splint, and find someone to go to his house and give physical therapy. Someone who wasn't her. Someone who'd never thrown her pride to the wind and herself at a man who had clearly never wanted her.

Or at least not thrown herself at this particular man. Someone who'd always known you can't rehabilitate the bad boy.

But if you were lucky, maybe you could rehabilitate his ankle.

There had to be at least one such physical therapist in LA.

Liam half fell into the first chair he saw inside the treatment room. Not a recliner. Foot still down. All the better should he need to make an escape, an idea that stubbornly refused to go away. And the idea of reclining made his stomach roll, much like the first summer together when they'd all gone to Six Flags. Fifteen, stupid, with something to prove…jumping on his first ever roller coaster right after gorging himself with junk food and a milk shake…

The world felt tilted enough, without a chair adding to it.

Grace clearly didn't want to see him. First time that had ever happened. After that night he'd stayed away, but before that night she'd always been happy to see him, full of smiles.

Maybe it was shock. He just had to give her a few minutes to compose herself.

Maybe this was a mistake.

Reaching as high as he had meant every new relationship came with a certain amount of danger—personal or professional, it didn't matter. Not necessarily physical danger—though that was an unfortunate reality too—but it seemed like everyone was looking to make a quick buck selling any celebrity gossip they could get their hands on. More than just trashy network shows looked out for celebrity gossip. Now private websites and every form of social media got in on the scoops. It astounded him how fast a celebrity could fall from grace.

Grace.

She might not want to see him, but he could trust her not to be one of those people. Even if they hadn't had a history, she worked for a facility that guaranteed patient privacy.

But with their history... *Damn.*

He shifted the messenger bag back onto his shoulder and himself out of the chair to make for the nearest recliner. Convincing her to help him would be tricky enough without disobeying her instructions right out the gate.

He barely got settled with the foot of the recliner kicked up before she came bustling in, once again avoiding eye contact. It didn't take an expert to read that body language. Avoiding eye contact was a sign of vulnerability or of trying to hide something—given the situation, what she wanted to hide was likely that vulnerability.

She ducked into an office off to the side, saying in

passing, "Let me just stash my stuff and I'll have a look at your ankle."

Half her words came after she'd left the room, projected to carry through the open door, and she hadn't so much as glanced at him on the way through. That never happened these days. Since he'd become someone to be seen, everyone wanted to see him.

Everyone but Grace.

The problem with having an elephant in the room… he couldn't decide if it was generally a bad idea to mention it, or if he just didn't know how to mention it right. All he knew for sure was that neither of them really wanted to mention it—the idea of even trying summoned another wave of nausea. If she couldn't even bring herself to look at him without the subject coming up, it really wasn't the time to talk it out.

"I appreciate you taking the time," he offered lamely. What would he say to any other medical professional in this situation? Just talk about the job. Pretend. He was an actor, for goodness' sake. Just talk. "I've got a movie opening, three premieres to attend, and all the promotion that goes along with that. This couldn't have happened at a worse time."

She stepped back out of the office, finally letting him actually look at her in something other than her bathing suit. The clothes she wore didn't flatter, but she still wore them well. Her black scrub bottoms sat low on those hips, occasionally giving him another glimpse of golden skin when she moved.

"What exactly happened?" She dragged a stool to the reclining foot end of his chair and sat down. Only then did she look at him.

Ignore the elephant. Focus on the ankle.

"I twisted it while running." He answered her question and then fished for the bag he'd stashed beside him. "There are X-rays in here."

She didn't take the bag, but she did take the hint. "Did the doctors say it wasn't broken?"

Her hands gently lifted his leg and she worked his shoe off, then began unstrapping the splint—the only thing that had been keeping him upright today. He tried not to wince but any jostle pinged like someone poking at a bruise. Annoying, but more capable of creating tension in his shoulders with the promise of bigger pain around the corner.

"They said it didn't appear broken."

"Okay, it could still be a minor fracture, but until it starts to heal it might not show up on film."

He'd heard the same thing yesterday. And though she was gentle, his hands locked into the arms of the recliner, braced and ready to pull his leg free, even if he had no intention of doing so. Being ready helped somehow, self-comforting actions he'd been reading on her since she'd focused on him in the pool room. She'd wrapped her arms around her waist like she could hug herself right out of the whole thing.

Liam had studied body language enough to read almost anyone if he spent enough time with them, but someone he had such history with...well, he'd been able to read Grace from the instant she'd recognized him.

The shock may have dulled now, but she was still a little afraid...of him or the situation. Either way, it couldn't be more wrong.

All the movement finally brought enough pain to rob him of anything else to say.

As she peeled away the layers of light brown elastic wrap, the extent of the swelling and bruising finally became apparent. She gave a low whistle and lowered his leg once more to the foot of the recliner so she could slide up the hem of his slacks. Her hands moved quickly and surely, but somehow she managed not to touch his skin the whole time she labored to fully unveil his foot and leg.

"You did a number on it. I'm not going to make you move your foot right now, but you really shouldn't be walking on this. It should be elevated with ice to help with the swelling." She reached for his calf, the first brush of her hand on his skin causing his gut to join in on the stiff tension knotting his arms and the rest of his torso.

Gently, she lifted his leg, craning her neck to look at the underside of his calf. There was soreness there, but there was something else in the feel of her cool, soft hands on his skin. It was nice, if you discounted the pain.

She felt it too. Her complexion had been leaning toward pale since the pool, but the first brush of her hands on his flesh brought color zinging back to her cheeks. She either felt it or suddenly just remembered her embarrassment—which was too probable for him to count on any silly theory about connections and strange touches.

His leg just hurt, and he was more aware of anything to do with it now. Even the fan in his bedroom ruffling his leg hair this morning had made him do a double take. The hair had felt like it had been six inches long.

"Does it hurt up here?" She lightly squeezed the top of his calf, up beneath his knee, looking him in the eye finally.

Liam shook his head, holding her gaze.

The pink blooming on her cheeks set off the rest of her coloring, and everything about her was golden—

from the light tan testifying to her active outdoor life, to the flecks of gold in her warm brown eyes. Her hair was darker than he remembered—she'd always spent so much time outside that her light brown hair had always looked sun-kissed, but now, wet and pulled back into a ponytail, it was hard to tell whether she remained the quintessential California girl or not.

"Slightly sore, but not actual pain," he murmured. The undercurrents and tension made things weird, just not weird enough for him to change his plans. Grace had to be the one.

"I can see you had it elevated right after the fall and blood pooled up the back of your calf. You're sore up there because you're black-and-blue to the back of your knee." She laid his leg down again, and then went on talking about the injury. Something about tearing or stretching tendons, and all he could think about was the contrast between black lace and golden skin...

She paused long enough that Liam looked back to her eyes. Was he supposed to say something?

"Did they say anything like that?"

"Like what?"

"Like surgery to repair it?"

"Surgery?" The word snapped his attention back to what she was doing rather than how she looked. "No. I really don't have time for surgery. I have a premiere tonight in town. Two more tomorrow—a big one in New York and a small, local one where the movie was filmed in Virginia. And then another day of interviews when I get back here..."

She sat back and looked at him over the tortured ankle, one brow lifted screaming *idiot* at him, even if she held off actually giving the word voice—he recognized that Watson family expression.

Get it together. This is business. He still saw one of the Watsons on a regular basis, which made this mental trip down memory lane ridiculous. He'd lost her six years ago, not six minutes ago.

"I know you can wrap it with tape to give it support enough to power through this," he said, lifting his foot away from her hands and putting the recliner arm back down. Getting upright would help. "That's why I came to you, Grace. You've worked with athletes injured mid-game, kept them playing and all that. Certainly you can work with me long enough to simply keep me walking for a couple of days. And then I will do whatever it is you tell me to do in order to recover. But right now...I need to play through this."

"Those athletes who get taped are only mildly sprained. They can bear weight, just need some extra support to keep up with their range of motion. This is not that kind of sprain. You need crutches."

God. Another person with the crutches. "No. No crutches. Athletes—"

"Don't use them on the court," she cut in, sounding irritated with him now. "I know, but I told you—this is different. And even if it weren't different, there's a big difference between taping an ankle before it starts to swell and after. And you're already terribly swollen. Tape won't do anything for you, it can't give you any support when there's an inch of gelatinous *squish* between the tape and the joint."

"There are medications that reduce swelling."

"Yes..." She sat back again and looked at him. The more they engaged about the injury, the more comfortable she looked. The blush had already faded to a hint of pink. Maybe the weirdness would abate if they just stayed focused on the work. "Diuretics are used for chronic conditions that cause water retention, and as preparation before a surgery that will cause massive swelling—mostly orthopedic surgeries. But not really for injuries like this."

"Can't we use them that way anyway? And ice? And elevation? Get the swelling down enough to tape it?"

"I don't know," she said, standing again, one hand rubbing her forehead. Another self-comforting technique—her embarrassment may have faded but she still felt the stress of the situation. "I don't prescribe medication. Let me talk to Dr. Rothsberg and see who I can find in New York to—"

She started to turn and Liam lunged to grab her hand. Instantly that feeling returned. Connection. Warmth. "Grace." He said her name. Maybe if he held her back with words he could let go of her hand. "Talk to Rothsberg about the medicine, please, but I came to you because I need you."

Her hand turned slightly in his, not so much pulling away, just giving the smallest slide of flesh on flesh. Every nerve in his hand fired and tingling heat spread up his arm.

Her hands were small but he felt the strength in them. So soft in his, and warmth he could spend a year studying… He found himself stroking her skin in return, his thumb making lazy exploration of the back of her hand.

Something else, he'd been saying something…but whatever it was left him.

They'd always had chemistry, but he'd never let himself explore it. He'd always kept touching to a minimum or carefully relegated to non-sexy situations for so many reasons, not the least of which had been loyalty. The senior Watsons and Nick meant a lot to Liam, but no matter how kind they were to him even Liam knew that would all end if he gave in to that lust that colored his vision every time he looked at her. Grace was off-limits, all he could have of her was his imaginings.

And this added a new element to the fantasy of the untouchable Grace Watson.

What would her hands feel like on the rest of his body?

CHAPTER TWO

GRACE STEPPED CLOSER to Liam's chair, her arm outstretched, hand captured.

How many times had this happened in her youth? How many times had hands clasped to do something mundane and helpful? How many times had her teenage self been sprawled on the grass near where Liam and Nick had hung out—doing whatever it was that teenage boys did—with her beside Liam just so she could beg for a hand up when it was time to go in for dinner? She'd used any excuse to make him hold her hand, even for just a couple seconds.

But it had always been at her instigation.

She'd been the one dying to feel her hand in his.

The only kind of flirting a dumb kid could come up with to try and make Liam see her as something other than Nick's kid sister.

And the least ridiculous, as it had turned out. When she'd hit eighteen and the time apart while he'd been at school had turned her desperate, her tactics had become the stuff that couldn't be lived down.

"I know you don't want to come with me," Liam said, his hand still in hers, even though he'd stopped stroking her skin now. It didn't really help clear her thinking, though.

She needed to make him let go. Get some space. Maybe her thinking would unfuzzy.

She took a slow deep breath and gestured back to the stool as she pulled her hand from his, indicating that she wasn't fleeing so he'd let go.

Please, don't mention it.

She might be able to force herself through this without having to face the embarrassment head-on, but if he wanted to talk about it…

He hadn't so far, but she could see it on his face every time she looked at him. Who could forget something like that?

"We haven't seen one another in a long time, I know," he said, nodding to his ankle. "Could you rewrap it? It feels better when it's got something around it."

"Yes. Of course." She grabbed the bandage, thankful for something to do, and began rolling it up to make the rewrapping easier. Focusing on a task was better than focusing on emotions that would make everything so much worse. Liam settled back again, his hands in his lap. She could still feel the weight of his eyes on her.

"I have no one else to turn to, Gracie. It seems that when everyone wants something from you, it gets harder to trust." The edge she'd heard in his voice drained away and he chuckled, sounding something like the old, charming Liam. The old Liam, the only one she'd ever let call her Gracie. "You probably hear some variation of that from entitled celebrities every day, whining about their success and how much it costs them."

He lifted his leg as she began wrapping, allowing her to pass the elastic wrap under and around his leg, snug enough to stop further swelling but not so tight that it would hamper circulation. Something she knew how to do, unlike the rest of this. And as painful as it looked, the physical pain was so much easier to deal with. And he really had hurt himself, but there were things that could be done to speed recovery. Things she could help him do after a few days of healing rest, but this insane plan to keep walking on it…

"I'm sure I could find someone skilled enough to help me through these next few weeks, but I'd have to keep my guard up, and that's really hard to do twenty-four hours a day. I know you're not going to secretly record me or take pictures to sell to the tabloids. I know you're not going to pay more attention to the limelight than to my recovery. And if I ever had any doubt, after seeing how badly you don't want to get involved… I'm certain of it now."

Her stomach bottomed out, hearing those words, almost as sure a hit as if he had mentioned the other. "It's not that I don't want to help you. I can see you need help and I'm sure you hate having to come ask for it." The words tasted of lies. She didn't want to help him, but none of that was his fault. It was her fault. He wasn't holding grudges and she wasn't either, but… "Maybe I could get you started and then after your premieres you could come back. That way I wouldn't have to let down my other patients either."

"James said you have a light enough schedule that the other therapists can cover it."

Of course he had. Because even if he'd known about their past, James would've still wanted to do what was best for the clinic, and that meant taking excellent care of the patients, not turning them away for wholly emotional reasons. Way more professional than her reaction had been.

She should just say yes, let him stop convincing her…

She opened her mouth to agree, but he was already saying something else.

"The Watson family has always been my safe place. There's no one I trust more than Nick and you. Even when the whole world felt barbed-wired and booby-trapped, I always knew I could come to your house and—"

"Okay, I'll come." She blurted the words out before he tried other guilt tactics. Guilt worked every time, especially since all of this awkwardness was her fault. He was the victim here. Heck, if the situation had been reversed and he'd come to her house in a trench coat and scanty underwear, it would've probably been considered a sex crime. And it definitely would've made all his other relationships with her family tense and awkward, maybe even worse than this.

It had been all on her and her childish fantasies that Liam Carter could've ever thought of her the way she thought of him. No. The way she *had* thought of him. The only thing she felt now was horrified at her own behavior. And desperate to never have to acknowledge or explain, to never experience that level of vulnerability again.

Holding the loose end of the bandage with her wrist, she fished fabric tape from her pocket and pulled off a strip to tack the bandage down before taping it more thoroughly.

"But, for the record, I was going to say yes before you added that little bit about trust and our childhood."

There'd been no way for him to win that situation, just like there was no way for her to win this one. No polite, professional, or *kind* way at least, and he deserved her kindness. She'd spent years trying to figure out what he could have said that would've made the rejection better at all.

Should he have just slept with her so she hadn't felt stupid about the hours of vigorous waxing and grooming to make herself irresistible? Wasted hours and needlessly tender post-waxing flesh…

"You mean I'm wasting my best lines?"

His question jerked her back from pondering the futility of her tender bits after that tragic home wax/shaving experiment. The smile she found when she looked at him softened the memories of bad razor burn and gut-churning humiliation.

"Was that a line in one of your movies?"

"Don't you watch my movies?" The words rang with obviously faked horror and he laid a hand over his heart as if the mere thought would do him in.

Silly.

Cute.

He was trying to make her feel better.

Before she could stop it, she smiled back. He certainly hadn't lost that natural charm.

But that kind of dangerous thinking had to stay as far from her scrambled gray matter as possible. The only way to get through this was to just focus on the injury, not the man. Not the way her insides expanded when he smiled at her, which they shouldn't even do anyway. Playful banter might as well be a sledgehammer, he could knock all sense out of her with one strategic swing.

She took a breath and eased the smile off her face.

Playful banter fit nowhere, it had to go for the next couple weeks.

Playful banter could make her forget.

Playful banter could make her stupid.

No playing with Liam Carter.

"When do we go?" Grace asked instead, bringing the conversation back on track.

"How fast can you pack?"

Grace strapped him into the splint, which at least was of excellent quality and slender enough that it could probably be hidden beneath his dress pants. "Driving home will take—"

"No. I mean whatever medical supplies you need. We'll pick up whatever personal items you need for tonight and the morning. When we get to New York, we'll get any restocking of supplies we need too."

"Your people will get whatever else we need, you mean?" She reached up to grasp the cuff of his pants leg and eased it back down over the splint.

"Yes." He smiled again, that lopsided, little-boy grin that always made her heart speed up.

She wouldn't smile. No smiling. Business didn't need so much smiling. Taking care of him didn't mean she had to have a sweet bedside manner, just a professional one.

"I'd rather deal with my own clothes, but for now I'm going to get some ice for your ankle, talk to James about whether a diuretic would be acceptable in this situation, and pack a quick bag of supplies. You sit here until I'm ready. The ice might do some good before you get back on your feet." Grace stood, heading to the freezer to get things started.

This day had certainly taken a turn for the bizarre and uncomfortable. And as stupid as it sounded to her to try and push through this, it wasn't her job to make celebrities behave rationally. It was her job to try and keep the damage to a minimum, and also the whole rehabilitation thing. She could keep him going for a couple of days if he could ride it out.

That was her job.

And swimming together, in or out of therapy, was right out. At least for the immediate future. The only way she was going to retain some semblance of her sanity around Liam was to keep The Trench Coat Incident as far from her thoughts as possible.

Grace settled into the forward-facing black leather backseat of the limo, dropping her bag onto the floor at her feet as she settled.

In the quiet interior of the car, the speed of her heart registered. She'd felt it before, hovering in the fringes of her awareness, but here she could hear the speed and analyze the force of the beast tangoing in her chest. It hadn't really ever come back down since the second she'd seen him standing beside the pool. He probably could hear it now, even sitting three feet away.

She fixed her gaze out the window.

It was still hard to look at Liam too long, even if she knew she was going to have to get used to it. The door shut behind him, and the darkened interior of the limo kept him from reflecting in the glass.

Finally, something going her way. Any brighter in there and the only place to keep from seeing him would've been the insides of her eyelids. And that never worked out, she was too good at seeing him there.

"So, about your clothes. You need to let me handle that."

If she had to look at him, it would be in bright, open places. And if she had to talk to him, it would be about strictly professional subjects, which clothing was not.

"I know I didn't have time to pack anything but medical supplies, but what I am wearing right now will serve for this afternoon. While you're at the premiere, I'll go home, grab some clothes and come back to the hotel."

"I have a personal shopper."

Out of the corner of her eye she saw him fish his phone from his pocket and flip it on. Two clicks later, he had it to his ear. Not listening to her at all.

"I don't need a personal shopper. I can get my own clothes." She tried again.

"They will be your own clothes afterward."

"Liam." She said his name, forcing herself to become reacquainted with the way it felt on her lips again.

Ten years ago, simply saying his name had made her happy. She would've sworn it even had a taste—a slick, plump fullness, luxurious and sensual, like her tongue sliding across her lips to suddenly find cinnamon chocolate fudge...

Now, instead of sweets, his name felt like rocks and sand in her mouth. Sharp. Awkward. Gritty.

"It's really not a big deal."

He listened well enough to carry on the conversation, but he clearly wasn't hearing her.

Ugh.

This kind of thing never happened to her. It probably never happened to anyone outside of *Cinderella* and *Pretty Woman*.

And that would make her the prostitute in this situation. Great.

Grace licked her sandpaper lips and took another purposeful breath through her mouth, because although the car might provide her with the ability to stop looking at him, it only amplified the heady cloud of good smells clinging to the man. His scent had been indelibly imprinted on her memories, earthy and rich, like salty air, old forests, and even older heartache. She found herself breathing slowly and deeply.

This was such a bad idea.

She was supposed to be acting professionally. Yelling at a client wasn't professional. And rolling in his scent was an extremely creepy reaction to being in his presence again.

Everything would be okay, she just needed to get ahold of herself. And maybe explain better, if she could come up with the words.

"I'm sure your personal shopper is lovely." Diplomatic. Good opening. "But that's not really the point. I already have clothes. I can take care of my own clothes. We're not going to be in another state until tomorrow so I have time."

He stopped participating in the conversation as someone had answered and now he was in full Hollywood mode, greeting and no doubt smiling.

Would he be doing this if she were anyone else?

"My other clients don't buy me clothing." She'd had some bring gifts, the kind that had made her feel awkward and—

"What sizes do you wear?"

The close confines of the darkened interior of the back of the limo felt entirely too intimate without him asking personal questions about her clothing.

She shifted to another seat to make room and redirected the conversation. "Turn sideways on the seat so you can stretch your leg out there. Any elevation will help with the swelling." Ice would have been more helpful, but she hadn't brought any.

A few seconds ticked by and she heard, "You're ignoring me?" Incredulity rang in his voice, making her want to turn and look at him.

Then again, everything made her want to look at him. He was singularly the most attractive person she'd ever seen in person—even years later and working at The Hollywood Hills Clinic, which was peopled daily with the beautiful and glamorous.

And her reaction to him was precisely the reason she needed to avoid looking at him excessively or, as it would probably be called, staring in a starstruck and creepy fashion. Though, admittedly, the more he banged this shopping drum, the less she felt like gazing at him like a lovesick cow, and more like smacking him in the back of the head.

Precisely why she needed to keep all talking strictly professional.

"I'm pretending you didn't just ask a c—" The word *creepy* nearly sprang out of her mouth, but she managed to stomp the sound down before she used unprofessional language. "It's really not workplace etiquette to ask those kinds of questions. So, just let me handle any clothing needs I may have on my own."

"We don't have time for this, Grace. I'd really rather you blend in, and the clinic logo and your name on your shirt do not help you blend in." A pause and he repeated into the phone, "I'd like her to blend in with the group."

His group—she was going to assume that meant his people, in the ol' I'll Have My People Call You scenario. So Liam called them his group.

"Right. Slacks. Blouses. Shoes. Accessories…"

Accessories. Of course, how could she forget accessories? She had accessories. She just hadn't thought to mention them.

"No. She's tall, but not six feet. Probably about a head shorter than me. Compact and slim, but not so much skinny as athletic. She's…"

He wasn't going to stop. Next thing he would be trying to describe her curves or ask her cup size, which would just bring that stupid trench-coat situation back to his mind. This was worse than just giving the fool her sizes. "Please, Liam." She tried his name again.

"I'll snap a photo of her and send it to you when we get to the hotel."

"For goodness' sake, stop!" Exasperated, she turned to look at him, holding out her hand for the phone. "Stop and I will text her my sizes."

"Him."

"Him! Whatever!" She held out her hand for his phone, her voice rising with her blood pressure. "I will text him my sizes if it will get you off this and get your foot up on that seat. Every minute it is down on the floor like that, it's swelling more. You know that, right, Superman?"

"Text coming," he said into the phone. "And the picture in a little bit. If you can have them at the hotel in the morning, we're leaving for New York at seven." He hung up before handing her the phone and turning to prop his foot up, as she'd all but shrieked at him.

Good thing she wasn't interested in seducing him. There was probably a reason that the low, velvety voice analogous with seduction was the opposite of a shriek.

A minute later, she double-checked the details she'd sent to Shopper Tom, as he was known to Liam's phone. If he picked clothing she hated, she'd wear it the one time and then find someone at work who wanted the clothes. They were temporary, just like this assignment.

The thought failed to comfort her, and she returned her attention to the window, thrusting the phone at him and settling back into her not-speaking routine. She couldn't display her freak-out voice if she wasn't talking.

* * *

In order to maintain security, and probably so Liam wouldn't be seen traveling with a woman whose shirt announced her position as physical therapist, the limo had gone around to the rear, private entrance of the hotel, where his group had met them.

Now, with him limping down the marble hallway in front of her—which no doubt led to the supremely classy yet neutral color-schemed heaven on the top floor—there was no room to doubt how bad an idea it was for him to be on the carpet tonight.

His three assistants bustled along with him, informing him how they'd set up the interviews. More walking, him making rounds to meet with reporters in different areas of the suite...

"That's not going to work," Grace cut in, and three sets of eyes turned to her. Liam's didn't, but his people had no idea she'd been complaining about him walking on it for at least ninety-seven percent of the time since she'd seen him. Mostly because it was a bad idea, and partly because she couldn't complain about what she really wanted to complain about...

"What would you like us to do?" Liam asked, stopping at a nondescript elevator and pressing the call button. Maybe he came this way all the time?

"One, you need to be off your feet as much as possible if you're going to have any hope of getting through the red carpet tonight. Two, you said you don't want this advertised. Which? You're limping like you've just suffered a back-alley amputation and are walking on a bloody stump."

He smiled at her description and then nodded to his people. "She's right. I don't want to walk any more than I absolutely have to."

Despite the smile he'd put on, there was a white ring around his mouth and his forehead glistened, though it was far from hot outside. Concealed pain. Ridiculous that he was so driven to conceal it.

But at least he wasn't arguing.

Their elevator stopped again at the very top of the hotel. "A suite, I'm guessing?"

"The whole floor." Liam nodded.

Naturally.

"Okay." The door opened to a tiny room with an ornate fancy door. One of the assistants handled the lock.

"Here." She thrust the rather large bag of medical supplies to the closest assistant, a pretty, petite thing who made Grace feel the antithesis of her name, and didn't pause to see if she could bear the weight.

"I'm helping you, Liam," Grace said, in what she hoped was a tone that brooked no argument. Even if she had to come back for the bag, she wouldn't have the thing smacking into him and upsetting his already precarious balance. A second later and she had his arm over her shoulders and her own around his waist, "If you have the whole floor, no one is going to see me helping."

A nod and he leaned, letting her take some of his weight, confirming how much his leg was hurting. As they made it into the suite, she began issuing instructions.

"We're going to need crushed ice, and find one of the rooms to set up and have the press people come here instead. We need a table, a chair, long tablecloth…and a footstool that can be hidden behind the fabric."

"Two chairs," the man at her left said, probably taking notes the way he rattled off her requests.

She turned Liam toward the closest comfortable-looking chair and kept arguing. "One chair. The reporter is going to stand. Or sit across the room. Or away from the table. Or levitate. I don't care. If they're at the table, they might bump his ankle or crash their feet into the stool. We don't want them getting curious for any reason and looking, right?"

"Right," Liam confirmed, nodding to a different chair to indicate his seat of choice.

A moment later, she had freed herself from the heat and natural cologne of his body to deposit him in the chair, his foot propped up on a table with a cushion padding the heel. "This will have to do until we get the other set up."

"Grace?"

She stopped and turned to look at him.

"Thank you. I suddenly feel like my brain isn't functioning at full power."

"When did you last take medication for pain?"

"I took something this morning."

"Any reason you can't take anti-inflammatories? Any kidney problems?"

He shook his head.

"Good. They'll help more, reduce swelling. I am also going to…" She paused and directed her attention back to the one remaining assistant. "Get some food up here. Also, the room you set up in should be close to a bathroom."

"Why?" Liam's question came from behind her.

"Because you're going to take a diuretic, remember?"

"Oh, right."

"And you don't want to have to walk a bunch to get to and from it." Having tasks to occupy herself with helped. Top of the list now: water. She detoured to the bar and came back with a fresh, cool bottle of water and, after she'd rifled through the work bag the woman had lugged in, fished out a few blister packs with the medicine Dr. Rothsberg had agreed to. "Take this. And this."

"What's that?"

"Potassium. If you take this diuretic, it will flush the potassium from your body. So you take it with potassium." At least he was still with it enough to ask the right questions and not just blindly take any medicine handed to him.

"The other? The pain medicine, it's not narcotic, right? Not the anti-inflammatory mixed with something you get with a prescription?"

There was a sound in his voice that made her stop and look at him, like a pinch or something else causing pain. It took her a second before she worked out why. His parents. How could she have forgotten about their addiction?

"No narcotic in it," she said softly. "It's a prescription-sized dose of ibuprofen, but we're faking it by taking extra over-the-counter versions of the same drug. Nothing addictive…" She regretted the word before it had even fully passed her lips. Some words had a chameleonlike ability to become hurtful depending on who heard them. With his history, and his recent addict ex-girlfriend… If she was going to be working with him, she'd have to be more mindful.

Before the statement could settle, or turn the room acid, she changed to what they needed to do. Work could always save them. "How long do we have to get you settled before the interviews have to start? And what time do you have to get ready for the premiere?"

One of the assistants, Tall, Blond, and Slight—or Miles, as the others called him—answered, "As soon as possible on the interviews. Most of the reporters are here already, and from there about four hours before he has to get dressed."

She stood a little straighter, knowing that her words were going to irritate them. "Okay, then make sure it's no more than two hours for the reporters. He needs a couple hours with his leg up higher than his head, and iced."

"Liam?" Miles looked around her to their boss.

"She's in charge this afternoon," Liam said, all but pulling the words from her mind. "And if we have to sacrifice a few angry reporters in order to put in a satisfying show on the carpet, then that's what we have to do. If you're worried, double them up. Bring in two at a time. Limit the number of questions they can ask. We can keep them moving. You gave them all the script, right?"

"Script?" Grace asked, zeroing in back on him.

"Miles puts together all the information that we want them to have, they hand out copies and that keeps me from having to repeat myself. Sometimes they want a direct quote in my own words and the copy we've handed out is wasted, but usually they are a good way of shortening interviews."

Miles added, "I'll limit them to three questions. Or maybe a time limit would be better. Three questions or...seven minutes."

"How many crews are there?" The math started sounding more than ridiculous.

"You don't want to know," Liam said. "They were planning to have four hours to do this, but I threw a wrench into things by going to The Hollywood Hills Clinic for you first."

And she needed to be there in order to intercede, but Liam didn't want people seeing her shirt. "Do you

have clothes here? Other than the ones for the trip and
the premieres?"

He nodded. "Why?"

"The crews are here and Shopper Tom hasn't had
enough time to get something here for me to wear.
Thought maybe I could snag one of your button-downs
and wear it instead of the polo until he gets here."

He nodded toward his female assistant. "Show Miss
Watson what's available in the wardrobe. The shirts I
wore when I leaned out for that role eight months ago
would probably work best."

Grace followed the woman.

He'd leaned out?

In general, looking at Liam's chest was a bad idea
if Grace wanted to keep her wits about her, but she
couldn't help herself now. His shoulders were broad,
had always been broad. How much weight had he lost
for a role? Everything looked normal to her with his
clothes on… What other tortures was he putting his
body through for this job?

What would she have put her own through to turn
pro? More than was sane. She'd done plenty during
rehab when she'd been hanging onto a shred of hope.
She had just never managed to get back there.

CHAPTER THREE

SOMEHOW GRACE HAD made herself the boss of Liam and his assistants, and Liam didn't have any desire to dissuade her from that course of action.

She got the crews in and out, and guarded the door in between. And the shirt she'd selected from his clothing didn't fit. Hell, it might as well be the only thing she was wearing for the way it distracted him. The collar unbuttoned deeply enough to tease at her cleavage, and the material tied in a knot at her waist, granting glimpses of solid abs and golden skin. No way would she be mistaken for a medical professional in that. She looked like his girlfriend or his lover, bossing everyone around and protectively fetching him water while still nagging him about this and that.

He liked that idea way too much.

But only because it was the perfect cover. No other options there.

If she didn't watch it, the story the reporters took away would be that Liam had dumped Simone and caused her to turn addict...so that he could shack up with the golden vixen managing his suite and tending to his needs while his assistants stood by and looked at her balefully. Yep, it all but screamed The Other Woman.

She escorted the fourth crew back and came back

to him, alone as she did every time. "How are you? Do you need a break before the next?"

"I do. I need to use the…facilities." He gestured. "And I won't ask you to stick around there, but someone to lean on would be appreciated."

"Just a second. I have crutches with me."

"You brought them anyway? How?"

She dug into the big duffel and started pulling out parts. Somehow, in that big bag of supplies, she'd managed to break down and stash a set of crutches. She flipped metal bits this way and that, pressed buttons, and adjusted the height. "Don't worry, when you're seated again, I'll stash them under the sofa so no one can see them. I just want you using them anytime you're not in front of the public. I'm serious, Liam. You are damaging that further every time you put your weight on it, and there is a window where you can get away with it, but past that it's going to heal wrong and you'll sprain it again. You'd be surprised by how little pressure a weakened ankle can withstand before it rolls out of the socket. Pain is a signal. It's supposed to dissuade you from acting like a he-man."

Arguing was futile.

"Fine. Give them to me. It might shock you to hear this, but I don't want to do more damage than I have to. I've rated it as high as I can beneath the top priorities."

She helped him get the crutches positioned right, and walked beside him toward the bathroom.

"What do you think you're going to have to give up by bowing out of these premieres and interviews?"

"It wouldn't take much to wreck the momentum my career has gained in the past two years. You know how the gossip is. You don't have to make huge scandalous mistakes for the climate to turn. People are already mad at me about Simone, and that's all speculation. I could keep making a series of small mistakes or demonstrations of bad judgment and the tide would still turn, just not as sharp a turn as if I went around punching people and biting the heads off live kittens."

He felt it before he even looked down and saw the face she pulled while walking beside him. She turned her lips in and bit them, the way she'd liked to do to hide smiles, or keep from saying something she shouldn't. Simone. She wanted to ask about Simone, how could she not?

No way. He wasn't up for talking about his ex with the woman he'd spent years comparing all his former girlfriends to.

"I know that's a silly example. What I want you to know is that I need to make the most of it while I'm in the position I've managed to reach. Do the most work I can, bank it for the inevitable downturn. And in the meanwhile get the best parts and stretch myself—increase the work that people think I'm capable of." He swung into the bathroom and turned to try and drill the importance of his words into her. "The next project is a really good one. It's also the kind of work that will keep me from being stuck in either the rom-com hero or action hero typecasts when I get too old for those kinds of parts."

She opened the bathroom door and waited for him to enter. "I'll wait out here."

It closed with a click and Liam shook his head. No comment on what he'd said. She thought he was being unreasonable just out of stubbornness. Or, worse, she thought it was ego. That his pride would sacrifice his leg if it meant the chance to prowl the carpet and be told how awesome he was.

He caught his reflection in the mirror as he passed it, scowling so deeply that he had to pause. Even speculating that she held him in anything but high esteem made him feel fifty pounds heavier, and it showed on his face.

Afterward, while avoiding looking into the mirror, he washed his hands and grabbed the crutches again.

"Door." He'd let her wait on him if she wanted to take it this far. "You think I'm being ridiculous."

"I think that you think you're invincible. I remember feeling that way myself, but when it goes? It's a really rude awakening."

"Liam?" Miles called from the door. "The media are getting restless."

"Right. Let me get settled and then bring in the next person. Wait at least ninety seconds." The crutches were awkward at first, but he'd played parts where they were needed in the past. His body remembered the way of it soon enough. He picked up speed to his seat, sat, and thrust them at Grace. "I'll take care of settling my foot with the ice on it."

His group were competent and cautious people and he even fully trusted two of the three of them, but having Grace take care of things felt the most secure.

When this was over, he'd have to make sure she knew how much this meant to him. Maybe she'd stop looking at him that way then. Maybe he'd stop looking at himself that way.

He should probably also give his group bonuses. He'd seen Miles—his longest-employed assistant—giving Grace the stink-eye at least twice today.

With a quick bend and tuck, she stashed the crutches beneath the sofa and out of sight. Liam made a point of not watching her bend over.

Twenty minutes and another trip to the lavatory later,

she was helping him back to the chair and paused to have a look at his foot before putting the ice back on it. "It's working. At least we have that. If the swelling keeps going down, your insane plan might actually work. Providing you can stand the pain. How's it doing right now, on a scale of one to ten?"

He could lie—and the professional side of his personality almost demanded it. If he told her that it was a solid four even when he was sitting still, and that it shot up to seven or seventy-five when he walked…

"It's pretty sore," he said, shaking his head. "And it is worse when I walk on it. The crutches are helping, but I'm only using them here."

"We've been over that," Grace said, heading toward the couch with the crutches. "But you didn't say a number."

"Three when I'm sitting." It wasn't really a lie. All these numbers were subjective. It just felt like a lie.

"And when you're on it?"

"I don't know. Six."

She straightened with a grimace and a shake of her head. "Before you go, if you insist on going, I'll give you a staggered dose of painkillers to help a little more. But you remember this tomorrow when sitting is a six and walking is a ten."

With the new rules limiting the number of questions they could ask, and doubling up on crews, they managed to get them all through with only a little extra time shaved off the required rest period Grace had given him.

And the remainder of it, all one hour and forty-seven minutes he'd spent flat on his back on the floor, his leg propped up on the seat of the chair he'd spent the afternoon in, his foot above the level of his heart, seemed like the easiest way to accomplish that.

However hard he'd thought it'd been to avoid her, he now fully recognized how much he'd missed just seeing her. Even considering the tension in their first minutes and the frequent flashes he saw in her eyes when she looked his way, things were going much better than he would have hoped.

She still thought he was being completely foolish, but she was getting him through what he needed to. And what he really needed now was another trip to the damned bathroom. Note to self: great for reducing swelling but lousy if you're not glued to the en suite.

"Grace!" he yelled from the floor. "Is my time up?"

"You have one minute, but I guess we can get you up early. Why? Do you need something?" She asked the question so innocently, he almost missed the teasing light in her eyes—small as it was.

"Uh-huh."

"Can you wait until I've had a second to look at it and tape it if possible?"

"Do we really need to delay? It's a quick trip."

"Yes, but any time with your foot down it's going to start swelling again."

And she'd made enough of a deal about it earlier that he didn't want to test her patience with him. Funny, he usually had a harder time letting go of his way than that.

"All right. If you can do it fast. Like in five minutes."

"I've taped on the sidelines. I can tape an ankle in under two minutes, but I need a couple more minutes to see your ankle once we've got the wrap off."

A minute later, she'd moved her supplies over and offered him a hand from the floor. "I thought you didn't want me to put it down."

"I want you to stand up and sit in the chair so I can tape it easier. You know, so I can get the tape under it without you having to strain to keep it off my lap and I don't have to give myself backache bending and twisting to get in past the seat back."

Liam shrugged and bypassed her hand. He could still stand up.

He sat up and flipped to one hip to push up off the floor without assistance, keeping what was left of his macho intact—or as much as it could be while hopping on one foot.

Sitting back down, he held his leg up and waited for her to make with the unwrapping, though really it was loose enough that she could probably slide it off like a sock at this point. He could only consider that a win.

When the skin was exposed, he prompted, "So?"

"So, this is not an instant decision. I'm going to need to move your foot around. I'm sorry, it's going to hurt, but I will try to be gentle. I need to make sure that what I diagnosed earlier was correct. Inversion sprains usually involve certain ligaments, and the method of taping is slightly different depending on whether it's the top one or the bottom one. I won't bore you with the names."

"So it can be taped? When you know the right taping procedure…"

She didn't answer yet, just gently moved his foot in the joint—pointed up, pointed down, side to side. It was the side motion that had him hissing loudest.

"Anterior talofibular ligament. And possibly the calcaneofibular."

"I thought you weren't going to bore me with the names."

"I'm just showing off." The tiny smile she gave came with a wave of relief in its wake. Almost normal. Her twisting his foot around might hurt enough that his jaw ached from clenching it, but physical pain could be borne much easier than what they'd been sidestepping since the second she'd pulled herself out of that pool.

"There's so much bruising I'm still not sure that there isn't actually a tear and not just too much stretching."

"Grace." He said her name a little louder, forcing her to stop what she was doing and look at him. "Can it be taped?"

"We're going to find out. I'm going to tape it, you're going to have people help you shave or whatever here in this chair, and keep it elevated until you absolutely need to stand up to get dressed. It might also be a good idea for you to—at the last minute—gently walk around the suite to try and get the motion down. When you've got your ankle locked, it changes the method of locomotion. Hip and knee flexing becomes more important. And it will also probably make your back hurt before too long, so don't walk any more than you absolutely have to."

Once more she went into that bag, this time coming out with an electric razor and some other supplies.

"I'll use my own razor when you're done."

"This isn't for your face. I'm shaving your leg."

"You are?"

"You want me to tape it?"

"Yes." He sighed and leaned back, letting her have her way again. "Just don't shave anything else."

"I'm not here for manscaping. I'm here to save your skin from the tape."

"Couldn't you just put something under it?"

"I am. But I use a light adhesive spray too so it doesn't slide and cause blisters."

"Fine, fine."

A moment later she had his foot cradled between her knees and was shaving halfway up his calf, all around.

Seconds only, and while it wasn't exactly a close shave, it got the job done. Then she hit it with the spray and grabbed a thin, blue stretchy wrap. It went on next, covering his leg from just below the toes, around the heel, and just over halfway up to his knee.

Grace hadn't been lying when she'd said she could do one in under two minutes, a wrap that would be tight and functional but maybe a little bulkier than she wanted. She'd take her time and do it in three or four minutes this time. After a couple of strips to anchor it, she flexed his foot up at a good right angle and laid down the stirrup strips. And then heel locks and figure eights of tape around the foot and ankle.

"How much tape are you going to use?"

"I'm going to make sure that none of the pre-wrap is showing except where the ends poke out a bit. No holes. It needs to be closed up completely or it might start to come off. So maybe the whole roll of tape. And maybe some other tape on top of it. I want to see you walk on it first. Then if we need the stretchy tape, we'll slap another layer on, just to add that little bit extra support."

He made some noise of affirmation, but stopped asking questions. Which gave her an opening. "I know you don't want anyone to find me out, but if I just go to the theater and lurk in the crowds by the carpet, that should be all right. I don't want to be up here sitting, waiting, when you might need me on the ground. I'll stand out of the way somewhere."

"I guess that's okay. I mean, you'll try to stand out of the way somewhere, but there's a lot of jostling that happens along the carpet. Not just from the cameras but also the fans lining up to snap pictures and shake hands. It's a big deal for them. If that happens, just go back to the limo and sit. I really don't want to have you helping me in public either. If I fall over, I fall over. Better that it looks like a fresh accident than something that I had to bring health professionals with me to manage."

"You really want to fall on camera?" she asked, hand fumbling in the bag beside her for the wide athletic tape.

Liam made a noise and shook his head. "But we're not talking about what I'd like, we're talking about what might provide the best public reaction. If I fall and limp off to the limo, I can just claim the doctor said I need to stay off it a couple days and that it will be fine, but if I am there with a physical therapist..."

"This is ridiculous. A fall is a fall, everyone will react to it the same way. They might even be happy that you're bringing someone like me with you in order to try and minimize the damage. Though I dare say that they'd strangle you if they found out that you're planning on walking on it unassisted in this condition. That might make them think you're out of your mind and incapable of the part. I know that's what would push me over the edge."

"You're a medical professional. And this is your job. Regular people, and especially people in the industry, want me to be a superhero."

"Is that what the part is for? A superhero?"

"No." He denied it too quickly, and for a man used to acting—basically lying for a living—he didn't pull the denial off at all.

"Your left eye just twitched." She stopped what she

was doing, though she hadn't really gotten started wrapping the thing yet. "It's *so-o-o* for a superhero. Who?"

"It's not what you think. It's different. He's a kind of medieval superhero, I suppose."

Before she could stop it, Grace felt her eyes roll and she scooted back and went to fish the crutches out. "Just until you get on your feet and have taken a few practice steps. Ease into it. Let your arms carry you until you find the right stride. And don't be afraid to call it off if you come to your senses."

Another moment without arguing. He took the crutches and carefully began to crutch-walk, easing onto the poor tortured foot. While he did that she got him the next round of over-the-counter painkillers.

"I think I want the stretchy tape."

"I think you do too," she murmured.

As bad as it was, the stretchy tape would add a tiny bit more support but it was kind of like painting the door when the house was falling down. But maybe it would help or have a placebo effect.

"I'll get it. You take these, and I'll send the anti-inflammatories with you. You can take them when the movie is playing—take water with you if you don't have drinks or whatever. I don't know how premieres are. Do they run the refreshments counter during one?"

He gave her a strange look but swallowed the pills down without water.

"Don't do that with the medicine. It needs to be taken with food."

"I'll handle it. Whatever is necessary to make this work. Now get out, I need to get dressed."

She handed him a blister pack with the appropriate dose, then headed for the door to the foyer area and yet more exceptionally tasteful shades of beige. She snagged her tablet as she walked out to where they'd been staging the reporters, out of sight of Liam and his crutches.

"Manage and document his dosing schedule so they can't screw it up, and add it to his chart." Along with his inability to heed much of her advice, and her rigorous objections to him walking on it.

Not that it would matter to anyone, but it made her feel a little better. The tablet accepted her words without argument.

Liam braced himself as the door swung open and he stepped out.

The first official step of the night, and it would have to be on his bad ankle. One thing he couldn't control was the direction from which cars arrived to drop off passengers at the red carpet. But it figured that he'd have to get out of the car on his bad ankle.

With a deep breath, he stepped down and used his arms as much as possible to haul himself from the car. Smooth.

Luckily for him, he had actually managed to control when he arrived, delaying his arrival until there were already plenty of people there to look at. Maybe the effort it took to get up would be missed.

Maybe the effort it took to keep his face a calm mask would also be missed. If he was lucky. But since his fall Liam had felt anything but lucky.

The gait that Grace had returned to his suite to demonstrate and practice was unnatural, but nothing he hadn't had to do before.

He had to use the hip and knee, propel himself forward with the other leg as much as possible to disguise

the fact that he wasn't really pulling off heel-to-toe locomotion anymore.

She had made it look easy. But she'd probably had to
do that walk a thousand times for other patients.

In this whole mess, she was the one bit of luck on
his side. Not just that she hadn't pushed him out of her
office immediately, and not even that she had agreed to
come with him—those were things he could actually
put down to James Rothsberg's influence as everyone
wanted to please their boss at least a little bit. But his
luck was that she still smiled at him on occasion.

After that night had gone down, at first he'd stayed
away, hoping to give her some time to get over it, but
soon enough he had been so busy with all the menial
gigs actors did to get by before their chosen career
began to pay off that he'd put checking on her at the
bottom of his list of things to do.

He'd been unable to ever ask Nick about how she
was.

Neither could he have asked Mr. or Mrs. Watson—
David and Lucy. Or gone directly to Grace either.

Eventually, giving her time had become just plain
staying away. And he'd kept busy enough not to do anything but acknowledge that the situation had made him
sad. There had always been another low-wage gig to go
to, until those low-wage menial gigs had become low-
wage acting gigs, and then higher-wage acting gigs as
his skill had increased…

The long hours of daylight meant that he had to do
the walk under the kind of light that mandated he use
those skills and give an exceptional performance now.

If it weren't for the amount of radiation he'd sucked
up being reassured that he hadn't broken it, and his desire not to have any more X-rays at present, he might go

back to the hospital and demand another set of films. How anything could feel this bad and not be broken was beyond him.

He'd known he and Grace had been broken by that night, but only here, in his own time, when she was no-where around since he'd forced his way back into her life, had he even realized that he was angry about it.

It had been there in his expression in the mirror, but he'd put it down to pain. But the truth was…as con-flicted as he had felt in that moment, and as guilty as he'd felt since then, he'd also felt anger that he'd lost her over it.

Not angry at her, not even angry with himself, just angry and frustrated.

No more than ten steps in and he'd been noticed. Cheers started in a wave, from the first to spot him, the advance warning system for the crowd, until it was all heads and flashbulbs.

And he could feel his brows furrowing. It wasn't the time for that, it was time for smiles.

This would be easier if…he didn't have to do it.

Wave. Smile. Stop for pictures. Shake hands. Don't show the pain grinding up his leg or the conflict churn-ing through his gut. It had all worked out for the best anyway, Grace deserved someone who could stay for-ever, and his relationships came with an already de-termined expiration date. Something he couldn't do to her, even if he could get past all the family conflicts.

When this was over, when he got back to the hotel, Grace would take care of him. She might lecture him, but she'd do it with her gentle hands and a level of ex-asperation that told him she still gave a damn. Even if the mortification of that night had stayed with her more strongly than he would have liked, she still gave a damn about him.

That was something to feel lucky about. Something to feel grateful for.

Even if it would make things harder.

CHAPTER FOUR

THE TIME BETWEEN Liam leaving and the time that Grace had managed to make it to the theater swelled to the point that now, despite the fact that she'd not arrived for forty-five minutes after Liam had, she wedged herself through the crowds enough to catch sight of him still working the carpet.

Granted, he wasn't running up and down the length of it, but he did move from one side to the other, shaking hands, taking pictures, signing anything that people thrust at him.

Shopper Tom, or as she called him now, Tom, had come barging into Liam's suite about three minutes after Liam and his crew had left, then had insisted on making Grace try on clothes to figure out what gave the best fit. Were these shoes the right size? Did these slacks ride too high at the hem to wear with the heels he'd picked up for her to pair them with?

Did she even know how to walk in heels?

What about this color?

How did she like blouses to hang—did she prefer a very close fit that showcased her figure or did she want to go for the old Hollywood style with flowing material?

Did she even know how to put her hair up in anything but a ponytail?

By the time she'd managed to usher him out of the suite she'd had a scalp-stretching bun forced on her, as well as more than half the clothes that he'd brought with him.

This nonsense was going to last two days. Two days. Not twenty. In two days, she'd be back home and in her own clothes, she wouldn't have to blend in with Liam's Group. She could wear what she wanted. She didn't need five pairs of slacks. She didn't need blazers and blouses, and why in God's name had Liam included accessories and shoes for every outfit?

Grace flexed her toes up and then gave them a wiggle in the strappy sandals she'd still managed to succumb to wearing with the suit—aka the last thing she'd agreed to try on. She didn't blend in. The crowd dressed casually. She looked like she'd come straight from closing down a tenement for the poor and disenfranchised. Or, actually, she probably looked like she was trying too hard to look important.

While Liam looked tired. And in pain.

And like he needed to be knocked out, since that apparently was the only way she was going to get him to behave and actually take some time to heal.

Anyone who watched him right now would likely come to the same conclusion. He tried, bless his little idiotic heart, but his limp was still there. Pain had a way of overriding willpower and concentration. It also distracted from a person's ability to judge anything accurately, like how well he was doing pretending it didn't hurt.

By the time he made it to the double doors and out of her vision, Grace's irritation had turned to worry and her head ached from the way her brows refused to un-pinch.

No matter where she stood in the crowd, she wouldn't be able to keep an eye on him now. The only thing she could pray for was that Miles, the assistant who hated her, would keep an eye on him and not let him overdo things.

As if that would happen. It'd mean going along with her demands, and if she'd picked up anything from him this afternoon it was that his last priority was pleasing her. Liam wanted to keep going, and Miles would facilitate that, regardless of whether or not it was best for Liam.

With a growing sense of dread she turned to push her way back through the crowds. They were sticking around to be there and see those shining people they'd come to see on their exit back out of the theater. One trip, two chances to catch sight of them, no matter if they had to stand waiting two or more hours in between.

Not Grace.

Let Miles help keep him on his feet. The trouble with having no control over a situation? No matter how much she told herself that he'd be fine, that he was an adult and could make his own decisions, she still worried about him all the way to the street to catch a taxi. And likely would continue to worry for the remainder of the night, while she sorted out only the clothes she'd wear in the next two days and lumped the rest together to be messengered back tomorrow.

But at least that would give her something to do besides fret.

Two hours later, Grace dragged the crutches out from beneath the cream-colored sofa. She'd intended on doing so when Liam hobbled in the door of the massive suite she'd been pacing since the ten minutes it had taken her to sort the clothes out.

But, amazingly, he'd called and asked her to bring them down to the back entrance.

She couldn't decide whether it was a good thing or a bad thing. Passing her bag of supplies, she grabbed it for the splint and implements stashed inside, just in case it was a bad thing.

A short ride down, and she hurried to the back entrance.

A small part of her wanted to believe this request for the crutches was a positive thing. That he had decided that he should do what she wanted, and had given up on whatever macho idiocy that had him feigning invincibility.

When she stepped out the back, the limo was waiting. He hadn't even hobbled inside without them.

Liam sat sideways at the opened back door, pale and slouching, his tie undone and his shirt half-unbuttoned.

"Good grief, you look horrible."

"Thanks," he muttered, glancing down.

His look led hers and that overwhelming urge to shake him reared up again. "Oh, God, Liam. Did you try to chew through this tape?"

"It's cutting off circulation, which I would have thought would make it hurt less. But it doesn't!"

She propped the crutches against the side of the limo and dropped to her knees, glad she'd brought the bag. It took only a moment to locate her gauze scissors and she slipped the safety end under the tape to cut through what he'd managed to make impossible to remove any other way.

"Did you tape it like a puzzle on purpose?"

"Yes, actually. I taped it like a puzzle on purpose because that's the way you get the best support without cutting off circulation. Unless you hobble around on a badly sprained ankle despite medical advice, make it swell up and cut off circulation anyway."

Pitting edema. It had swollen so much that the scissors left a groove down his leg as she cut and tugged the tape away. "If you just keep going around and around with tape, it gets far too constricting. I taped it specifically to support an inverse sprain."

He grunted in response, but that sound became a low, pained hiss as she got the last of the wrapping off and blood rushed back into the skin.

It hurt when the blood got back into the area too.

She tilted her head to try and see the damage, but the low lighting didn't make that possible. Examination would have to wait. "Let me get the splint on."

"No!" He couldn't snatch his foot back from it, but he did lift it. "I'll use the crutches and hold my foot up. I won't put any weight on it. Just don't touch it until we're back upstairs."

"You don't mind if anyone sees it?"

"We'll go fast."

Grace shrugged, grabbed the debris and stuffed it into the hands of one of his assistants, handed the bag to another, and rose to help him up on the crutches. "Don't go fast. Go slowly. I've never seen anyone else come out this way, have you? It'll be fine."

Once inside, the light let her see just how pale he was. He almost looked like he'd been dusted with white powder, like an extra at King Louis IX's court.

She wouldn't nag. Wouldn't yell at him. She'd just get him upstairs, tie him up and refuse to let him go to New York tomorrow. Yeah, that was a plan.

The look he gave her as he leaned against the inside

of the elevator let her know that her yelling wouldn't do any good anyway. He had the look of a man who'd been converted. In fact, the labored breathing and shaky hands said he'd probably have asked her for a wheelchair if there had been one in the suite.

By the time they got him upstairs, whatever civil facade he'd been putting up crumbled and no sooner had the door closed than he was announcing, "Everyone out. I need space."

Miles and crew turned right around, Hailey dropping the bag she'd carried by the door on the way back out.

What did that mean for her? Should she go?

Grace stepped back and gestured to the bar. "I've got ice waiting. Do you want me to help you get situated before I go?"

"You stay," he muttered, and continued through to the bedroom, which was elevated by a few deeply carpeted steps.

With the way he shook, Grace didn't trust him to navigate the steps on his own and scrambled along with him, hands at his back, ready to grab and lower him to the floor if he started to go.

"Stop. I'm fine."

"You're not fine. You're shaking hard enough for it to measure on the Richter scale. And you were using your foot for balance when it was splinted or wrapped. Now you're just a walking tripod. And I know how to control falls. I do it all the time. So shut up and take the steps. I'm not going anywhere. Be glad I don't have you by the belt. Yet."

He stopped at the foot of the steps and looked over his shoulder, "Your hovering is going to make me fall. Step off. If I fall, I fall. I'll roll the other way and protect my foot."

"No." She turned his head to face forward. "Looking back compromises balance. Move it, or I am going to do a fireman's lift and carry you up there, if for no other reason than to prove to you I'm not a delicate flower who can't help you."

"I'm just doing this to save your fool back. We can't both be laid up." Liam shook his head but took the steps as directed. Despite the bone-deep shaking in his frame, he got up them with ease and went to flop on the end of the bed. "You want to help me? Take off my pants."

Grace stopped in her tracks, her hands going to her hips as she regarded him. However pained and cranky he felt right now paled to the irate tilt of her head as she looked down at him. "Your hands work fine. Take off your own pants."

He unfastened them and then looked up at her, giving his best pitiful but harmless look. "Come on, Gracie. Don't make me stand up again. All I want to do is kick back, take some flavor of painkiller, eat, and sleep. And maybe ice it once it stops throbbing…"

"Fine. If you're going to play imbecile, I'll help you with your pants."

"Don't you mean invalid?"

"Nope, I'm pretty sure I meant imbecile. I went to the theater. Even with your limp it shouldn't have taken more than five minutes to make it the length of that stupid carpet, but I didn't leave here for forty-five minutes because Tom came by with clothes and made me try them on."

She hooked her fingers in the belt and tugged as he lifted with his good leg. He fell back on his elbows and watched her toss the trousers over her shoulder as she knelt to get a look at his foot. God, that thing hurt. If she touched it, he might cry like a baby. Maybe then she'd give him a little sympathy rather than her anger.

"Liam Jefferson Carter! What did you do?"

Uh-oh. The middle name had come out. She wasn't even going to pretend not to be furious.

One cool hand cupped his calf and lifted, contrasting with the fire in her eyes. "You know, I was thinking we might switch you to heat—ice is usually only for the first forty-eight hours after the injury, but it's worse now. That's why it hurts more, that's why it swelled despite the tape. Might as well be a new injury."

"I know," he muttered. "I'd actually say it hurts more right now than it did when I fell. So, congratulations, you were right. But you know I wasn't doing this just to be a pain in your butt. I have to, Grace. That's what this life is, if you're lucky enough to get this high, then your whole life is schedules and obligations, and when I sign a contract to do a movie I also sign on for the promotional aspects at the time of opening. It's contractual."

"And is it also contractual that you go in there without any support? You could have done this a lot better with crutches, Liam. Then you would still have met your obligations."

"No, I couldn't."

"Tell me why. Tell me exactly why, because..."

He lay back fully on the bed, pinching the bridge of his nose as if that would dispel his headache. The whole night had taken him to the end of his tether, so if she didn't get off this, he might kick her out with the others. Then he could sleep and let tomorrow worry about itself.

"Liam."

"I don't need a lecture. If you're going to keep after

this, then you maybe should just go to the other room. Or your own room."

"We didn't get me my own room. I've been here all the time." She straightened and leaned over the bed, looking down at him.

He couldn't deal with this right now. "Then we'll get you a room."

Just when he was about to scoot up the bed to reach the phone, she touched his face and stopped him.

That warmth again. She slid her hand to cup his cheek and his frustration all but left. And with it his ability to care whether or not he should enjoy her touch. It comforted him. It meant she still cared, and this wasn't just a job. She cared about him. And it felt good, he felt better.

Closing his eyes, he tilted his head into her hand and held it there with his own hand.

"Liam?"

"Shh. Just wait…" he said, not opening his eyes, just letting the warm strength of her hand soak into him.

Her thumb stroked his cheekbone in a soothing arc. "Tell me why it's so important. I need to understand this if we're going to keep working together. Because right now I know you're frustrated and in pain, and it isn't just hard to see you hurting yourself like this, it makes me feel ill. If you want me to stay, tell me why you have to do this."

He wanted her to stay. Hell, he wanted her to stay right there. Or maybe put his head in her lap and stroke his weary brow. That would be nice.

But staying was actually important for more reasons than his hedonist tendencies.

It wouldn't matter if he gave her what she'd asked

for. This was Grace, not someone who'd use the information against him.

"I'm starting another project in a few weeks—a part I've been dying for—and I don't want the producers to think that I am going to slow down production. It was between me and one other, right down to the wire, and they went my way. If I show up limping around now, they're going to reverse course." He opened his eyes and looked into hers, and then slid her hand from his cheek to his chest but kept holding it there. "We haven't even signed the contracts yet. It's all verbal agreements until there's a signature on the dotted line. And even then sometimes contracts can be broken."

"What's so special about this part?"

"It's a book…" With her hand in his and her eyes fixed on him, he could tell her why. Maybe not everything, just give her an idea. "Sit here with me." He patted the bed and transferred her hand to his other one so she could sit.

When she had, and turned her hand over to wrap her fingers around the edge of his palm in return, he took a breath to steel himself.

"Don't laugh."

She shook her head, squeezed his hand.

"Do you remember, well, your parents would just come home with little gifts sometimes?"

She nodded, still not speaking.

"The book was the first time… I'd been hanging out at your house pretty much every day for about six weeks, and then one night they came home from work and had stopped at a bookstore. Lucy got you some book you'd wanted—I don't remember what it was—but then she reached into the bag and pulled out two copies of another book, handed one to me and one to Nick."

"Mom liked to do that—still does that, actually. Now they're making that book into a movie and you want to be in it?"

She didn't get it, but he could see in her eyes that she was trying to.

He might be able to explain, but he couldn't do it while looking at her. Letting his gaze fall to where their hands joined in his lap, he tried again.

"It was the first time anyone ever gave me a gift for no reason. Birthday and Christmas presents were real hit-and-miss with my folks, depending on what they'd done with their money that week. It wasn't really about the book. I was just included, like I was an extra son who'd sprung up and was automatically accepted. So… it was the first time I had any idea of what it was like to be in a family."

When he looked back at her, her eyes were damp and she was silent, clearly working through what he'd told her, and the implications of it all.

"Plus, it's outside my usual roles, so it's kind of a big deal career-wise that I have this part, Gracie."

Lifting her free hand, she swiped her eyes quickly and nodded. "Okay." Accepted. "I'll do whatever I can to help you, but understand something for me?"

He turned just a little to look at her better but kept her hand in his.

"It doesn't just anger me that you're causing yourself more pain, but I'll try to ignore that as much as I can. I'll help you do what you need, but please take pity on me, and make all these things you have to do as easy on yourself as you can. No unnecessary walking. Put your foot up anytime you can."

"Come with me to the premieres tomorrow." He said the words before he'd really thought about the urge.

But the desire was real. He hadn't been at his best on the carpet tonight, and not just because of the ankle. He'd also kept wondering what she was doing. Just how angry she was with him.

"I thought that my coming with you to the premieres was what this was all about?"

"No," he said, letting go of her hand so he could move around her and his foot was propped up on the bed beside her. "Come as my date."

She opened her mouth to say no, and he held up a hand, energy coming from some unknown source to give his words some urgency. "Every time I've gone solo to a premiere or event, I end up doing way more walking around. Come with me. Be my date. Keep me with you and I won't do as much walking."

"I don't know. I don't have a gown or anything."

"Tom can fix it."

"It's late, he'd have to do some night shopping or very early morning. We're leaving at seven, right?"

"Yes, but he can do a lot from the plane. He's got numbers for both coasts. We'll go to New York and then take a short flight down and back from Virginia. He can have prospective gowns waiting for you. And whatever you need to help get you ready."

She didn't look convinced. The furrow in her brows could be doubt or worry. What would make her come around?

"You can be my walking stick. So I can lean against you a little and not put weight on my bad leg when we're not walking."

Her frown deepened. "Will you use a cane?"

"If I have you, I don't need…" Her look stopped him. "I'll carry a cane if Tom can find me something that could look like an accessory. And then I can use it if I need to."

The frown stuck and he caught her hand again, looking for any way to make it sound plausible. "You know, the movie is a historical. Gentlemen used canes. Maybe I could play it as a nod to the movie and theme."

"You just thought of that now?" Shaking her head, she pulled her hand free. "Where's your phone? I need to call Tom if we're going to do this."

He pulled off his jacket and handed it to her. "Inside breast pocket."

She hung the jacket on the back of a chair and retrieved the trousers she'd thrown on the floor. "Scoot up to the head of the bed. I'm going to talk to Miles about the travel stuff and call Tom. You order dinner—the phone is on the table."

He could do those things. Scooting up hurt, but he could do it.

She walked to the door, dialing as she went.

When he'd asked her to help him out, it had never occurred to him that she'd have to do so much for him, but it was like a godsend, having her here.

He hadn't thought about telling her about the project earlier. He knew it was silly and sentimental—there could never be resolution with all the dark parts of his childhood, even if the role felt like giving a gift to the child he'd been. A kind of resolution. His parents were dead and gone, so there couldn't be any peace from that corner, but David and Lucy had been the only real parental figures in his life.

And Grace...he could make things right with her. He could make their tentative friendship a real friendship again. Talk it out. Maybe it was time to talk it out now that she'd grown comfortable enough to yell at him. That had to be some kind of sign.

He just had to think about what to say, make sure that he planned it out and didn't do anything to make things worse between them.

Tomorrow. He'd think about it tomorrow. Tonight he'd eat, do whatever she told him to do, and tomorrow, when some of the pain had abated...

CHAPTER FIVE

"WHAT TIME ARE we taking off?" Liam asked, leaning back in his seat with the foot rest raised.

The private jet loaned to him by the studio had all the bells and whistles, and none of the executives—both of which he was thankful for. The circle of people in the know was already large enough between his crew, Grace, and Tom—who'd been sworn to secrecy about the ankle situation and seemed happy to go along with the ruse.

"We're supposed to take off in fifteen minutes." Miles's voice came from the seats behind where he and Grace sat.

Grace had the ice back on his foot, and she'd managed to get another couple of diuretics from James. Liam looked up at her. "Shouldn't I take one of those swelling pills again?"

"Not when you're flying," she said, settling into the seat beside him.

Despite the understanding they'd reached last night, she still didn't look happy with him or being there.

"Why not?"

"Being dehydrated on a flight increases the chances of a blood clot forming. Really, you should be drinking more water right now, especially since your mobility is lessened—you can't get up and walk around much, and you can't put weight on that ankle to flex the muscles well enough to—"

"But I'm not dehydrated right now. I'm just overly hydrated at the ankle. And our window between when we arrive and when we have to get ready is small."

"I know. We're doing the best we can."

"I'll risk it."

"No."

"Grace, it took three hours last time to get the swelling to go down."

"I know, but we'll just have to try and make it work. Maybe keeping your leg elevated on the flight will help it."

"It's not that elevated."

"You can lie on the floor after takeoff and put it on the seat again if you want to."

"It takes an hour to kick in. You want me to compromise on things? You have to compromise too, Grace."

Shouldn't she be happier with him now? She knew this wasn't just about ego.

"I will, when it's not life-threatening levels of dangerous." Her mouth said yes, but the shake of her head made him doubt she meant it. "Just relax for now. You have a long flight, and I know you didn't sleep well last night. Maybe you can sleep now that the worst of the pain has passed."

"I doubt it."

"Well, I have a way to pass the time if you're all done fighting," Tom, the middle-aged stylist, snapped at Grace, and pointed to the front of the plane. "I need a few pictures of you."

Grace made a face. "Liam sent you a picture yesterday and I'm here in person today. Have you deleted the picture already?"

"No, but that was one angle, and it was from behind. I was flying blind on what your chest was like until I met you last night."

"And now you've seen it."

"He saw your chest?" Liam asked, frowning dramatically, wanting to cajole her out of her glowering a little. "That hardly seems fair. I'm the one footing this shopping expedition."

"He didn't see-it see it." Grace made an annoyed sound, unbuckled her seat belt and went to stand where Tom had directed. She suffered through a series of photographs as he had her stand full front facing, then three-quarter profiles both left and right, and then again from the back, and three-quarters profile back…

By the time they got to the last couple of photos, her hands were on her hips and she repeatedly took deep, disgruntled breaths.

"You're very pretty to be so camera-averse," Tom mumbled, letting her off the hook with a gesture for her to go back to her seat.

"I don't even want to know why I did that," she muttered, buckling back in beside Liam.

"You're probably lucky he didn't have you strip down to…" The statement died in Liam's throat.

Since last night he'd been mentally working through ways to bring up that trench coat, but that was not the right way to do it. Especially here in front of everyone.

The hint of color creeping back into her cheeks confirmed that her thoughts had gone to the same place. He had to say something else to drag her out of it, so he went with the real explanation. "He's probably looking at gowns on his tablet and some books. He wants to see you in the right profile so he can easily picture how a dress would work for you."

"I guess." She reached for a magazine stashed on the wall beside her seat, shutting the conversation down.

But if that look she'd given him was anything to go by, he had an inkling how she was going to react. Not great, but maybe if he did this right, it wouldn't be so bad.

"Body frame is very important when it comes to the style of a gown," Tom confirmed.

Just another reason he didn't want to talk about this all here. The small cabin made it possible for everyone to hear every word. They didn't need all their issues on display, this uneasy alliance was already juicy enough.

But he didn't want to dance around the subject anymore. She didn't need to know all the gritty details but he could apologize. Tell her it wasn't a reflection on her that he had sent her away. Remind her about the loyalty and kinship he felt to her family that kept him from considering her as anything other than a friend. She didn't need to know the other reasons, the ones that made up the bulk of his present resistance.

So he'd tell a lie. But a white lie. A lie he wished was true. The loyalty part was there, but it still didn't help him not consider her as anything other than a friend. He considered, he considered so much that sometimes he even got confused about who they actually were. It just wasn't a situation he could pursue.

He'd spent years thinking of the incident in the only way he could minimize it: she'd been embarrassed but had then probably put it from her mind and moved on. Thinking about it any other way left him angry with nothing to fight against.

Twenty-four hours in her presence had brought a few

other revelations he might never have come to on his own without seeing her again.

This mess wasn't about her feeling humiliated because they'd both wanted each other but couldn't go there.

She thought she'd been alone in that desire, and that's what hurt her. If that were the case, it meant she hadn't been smart enough to read him right. It labeled her dumb, clueless, or cocky that she knew but didn't care how he felt about the matter. Mostly, in every incarnation of the situation where she felt alone in the desire, there was no making it better.

He'd have to tell her that he'd wanted to drag her to bed and that even now, years later, it had been the sexiest night of his life.

Then tell her that nothing could happen because of his loyalty to her family. If they were both shutting down the attraction with good reasons that had nothing to do with desirability, that might take the edge off the situation for her. It would help him were the situations reversed.

Last night's conversation about the book had been way too revealing for his peace of mind, but maybe that reason was something she'd accept now. He just had to come up with some way to make this all right.

There were very few good things about never pursuing real, lasting relationships—but the one thing he would change right now was not having the tools to instantly know how to fix this. All he really knew was that he had to try.

When they were alone.

The pilot's voice broke into his thoughts, announcing their clearance for takeoff. He had five hours to come up with the right words. And three hours to start hounding her for that other swelling pill.

"The wrap is getting looser," Liam said, gesturing to the foot he still had propped up on pillows piled atop the footrest.

The jet had just landed, and they were currently taxiing away from the runway.

She stashed the last magazine back in the rack and leaned over to look at his foot. "The pill is working already."

"Oh, it's working..." he murmured, doing his best not to give her anything else to be angry about. All this nonsense, as she referred to it, didn't make him happy either. He was getting his way, kind of, but it was hitting home that his way was stupid.

"I hope it means that some of the bruising is dissipating. Seems like that might make sense, there's blood pooled there, and fluid is being whisked away by a medicine. Maybe it will take some blood with it. I really don't know if it works that way, but it would be nice if it did. Might take some of the soreness," she said, then turned in her seat to look at Tom. "Did you find a good cane for him to use and pretend is just for show?"

"I did. I have a friend in antiques, he called around and found something nice and the right length. It has a sword hidden in it."

"So, if we're set upon by bandits, I can defend you." Liam smiled at her. She might not be trying to talk him out of his plan at every turn now, or telling him that it was stupid, but their conversation definitely hadn't diminished her surliness over the situation.

"I think it's more likely that if we're set upon by

bandits, they'll be aiming to kidnap you. Ransom you for shiny baubles."

And she was grumpier the closer it got to the premiere.

"Is there any way you can do the carpet prowl thing and then come back here and skip the actual movie?"

"We'll skip the early movie in Virginia, go strictly red carpet, then fly back to New York," he answered quickly, then redirected her attention back to his ankle and away from worrying about tonight. "The bandage is loose enough to feel irrelevant. Think you could wrap it again before we disembark?"

She leaned over to look out the window. "I guess there's no flight attendant to tell me to stay buckled in until we get to the gate. So, sure."

She unbuckled to head for the other side of his seat. He watched her flick the tape off and then unwrap the loose dressing. "How does it look? Think you can still tape it like before?"

"It doesn't matter if I should or not, but if the swelling continues to abate, we'll tape it. I'd be happier if it were also in the splint."

"I think my ankle feels a little better." He changed the subject to something that he hoped would ease her. She hadn't smiled the whole trip. Even when he'd assured her that it certainly felt better than last night.

It made him feel better at least. Reviews had come out that morning before the flight, and those had made him feel good too. Good enough that even if his ankle was hurting, he'd make the premieres.

The cane would help.

Having her there would help.

Two separate walks would not help, but it had started

to look possible that his foot wouldn't actually fall off and leave him with that bloody stump.

Now, if he could get any clarity on the trench-coat situation…

Liam's ringing phone echoed inside the back of the car sent to fetch them on the tarmac. Miles sat in the front with the driver, leaving Hailey and Dexter behind to get the luggage from the jet and catch up, and Grace all alone with the Sexiest Man Alive.

"You just turned it on. Does it send a homing signal for people to call you when you turn it on?" she asked. As soon as the words were out of her mouth she regretted them. Her mood had to improve. How many women would kill to be Liam Carter's red-carpet date? But every time he looked at her she felt like he was going to bring up that night. He hadn't, thank goodness, and he'd given her no real indication that he wanted to. Every instance when something had been said that might lead into that conversation, he'd changed the subject too.

She should relax.

"I think so."

He answered the phone and began talking. Reviews. Good reviews. Or what she'd call great, at least the ones she'd seen before they'd got into the air. And she had seen no mentions of his limp. So maybe he was right. Maybe she only noticed because it was her job to notice.

Tonight was the last night that he'd have to be on that ankle, and then tomorrow she'd get to go home, only see him at the clinic for treatment, and soon enough that would be over too. She'd get her quiet life back.

Today it was easier to look at him. Something had

transpired between them last night when he'd held her hand to his cheek and made his soft confessions.

The king-sized bed in his hotel suite would have comfortably slept them both, without either of them ever touching one another or even realizing that they'd been sharing a bed probably, but it was a move that Grace hadn't been able to accept.

Even though he'd offered.

Even though she'd slept on the couch and had got up every two hours for twenty minutes to wake him and ice his ankle.

Staring was bad. She forced herself to look back out the window. It was safer.

Even though she'd undressed him. Actually, the undressing was probably a big part of why she said no. Yes, he had been in his underwear in front of her, and that was similar to the outfit she'd worn at the scene of the Big Rejection. But things had been different. He was confident in his body, because… Damn. They had him shirtless in every movie for a reason, and it wasn't to display the dramatic black tattoo wrapping around one shoulder and crawling down the arm.

She became aware that the pitch of his voice had changed, and then began actually listening to the conversation. "Yes. I have an injury, but it's really not that big a deal. I twisted my ankle the other day on a run. It's…"

He paused and listened. When she made eye contact, his scowl communicated enough: she was wrong. They cared. They cared a lot.

"Is that your agent?" she whispered.

He nodded, mouthed, "Conference call."

So it was more than his agent. He squirmed in the seat, trying to find a more comfortable position. This car was much smaller than the one they'd used in LA. He could put his leg up, but he'd have to drape it across her lap.

Which might be uncomfortable for her, but it was better than him having it down, undoing all the good work the diuretic was trying to do. She waited to catch his eye and patted her lap, and whispered, "Put it up."

"I have my physical therapist with me. Actually, she's making me put my foot up right now, and she has been icing it and giving me the necessary medications since yesterday." As he spoke, he swiveled and put his leg across her lap. "You don't need to speak with her. I can answer your questions."

Why wouldn't he want her to talk to them?

A small argument ensued and he held the phone out, his expression grave. "Craig wants to talk to you."

"Is that your agent?"

"Yes."

"Who else is it?"

He listed several names and their importance, producer, director, blah-blah-blah.

She took the phone and answered questions. Who was she? Where did she work? What were her qualifications? It was like going to an interview for a job you already had, but once they got through the litany of questions they topped it with, "What's the diagnosis and prognosis for Carter's recovery?"

"He's got an inversion sprain. It's not the worst or the best one I've ever seen. It will heal and it's unlikely that he'll have much trouble with it in the future. We'll be starting actual therapy in a couple of days, once we're back in LA. Right now, I'm taping him and keeping him mobile."

* * *

Liam didn't watch her speaking. She sounded confident but, then, she was a pretty together person. She was also the only person, besides him, as bothered by the amount of stress he was putting the injured joint through.

Would it be better if he could hear their questions or worse?

"Yes. We'll return to The Hollywood Hills Clinic and start his physical therapy in a couple of days in the pool so he can start working on motion and strengthening without the need to bear weight.

"In three months? I doubt there will be lingering effects, but in three months, if he's having trouble, it would be as simple as taping the ankle before he does anything that might make it roll out. There are some pre-sized tape kits that come with two to three wide, sticky strips, and, when they are placed appropriately, entirely concealable.

"Yes. Colored and those that are a medium tan color, which would blend in with his skin tone. But I expect if you really wanted to conceal them, your effects people could do a light airbrush to… Yes. Yes. He'll be on the carpet tonight. I'm going with him and he's using some support in the form of a camouflage cane." She sighed. "No, it's not got a camouflage pattern. It's there to look useless but be useful."

"A prop," he whispered.

"A prop," she dutifully repeated.

There was another break in her answering questions directly related to him, where she listed several athletes she'd worked with and fished her phone out of her bag to thumb through it. "If it will make you feel better, I can provide references. Aside from Dr. Rothsberg, I can put in a call to former clients and have them call you if you need it."

Another moment and she hung the phone up and handed it to him. "You owe me. They know, they are convinced it's no big deal, and you can use your crutch at the premiere."

"Cane." He took the phone back, correcting her lest she get more ideas. She'd just told them cane, and if he showed up on crutches now, they'd need more reassurance. "Why didn't you tell them I'm the worst patient you've ever had?"

"Because you're not. You're just the worst one that I cared enough about to yell at."

Two minutes, that's what she'd said five minutes ago.

Liam leaned against the wall beside the elevator, all his weight shifted to his good leg.

This was the other thing that happened whenever he took a date to a premiere: waiting.

Just when he was about to send Miles after her, the door to the room adjoining his opened and Grace stepped out.

Or backed out.

There was some jostling of material and some muttering, which dispelled any doubts about who was in the gown, if he'd had any.

Pink? Flesh? Sparkly...silvery beige? What color was that thing?

When the gowns had shown up two hours ago, Liam hadn't even looked at them, just sent Tom to Grace with the garment bags and boxes of shoes.

"Are you going to come with me, Gracie?" he called. "Or are you going to stand there muttering at your skirt for the evening?"

She moved, shifting from the low light of her doorway into a halo of golden light from above, looking over her shoulder toward him as she did. The back was modest by most standards, bare shoulders and supple golden skin to the mid-back. Sexy. Understated.

Her eyes found his, deep and full of contradictions. Worry. Sweetness. Promises he had no business even considering.

Liam's heart stopped in his chest and then launched into a fast, skittering beat.

Gathering the front of her dress, she turned fully and let it fall, hitting him with the full effect.

Beautiful women in glamorous gowns were like Tuesdays in Liam's life. But he'd never seen anything like this.

"We have to go, Miss Watson," Miles called. Herding Liam toward his obligations was part of his job but even with his ankle aching he didn't want to hurry her. He wanted to look at her. Far away. Close-up. All the steps in between.

She still hadn't smiled at him, and he wanted it. The grumpiness plaguing her had been replaced by nervousness. She'd turned her lips in and chewed at the inside. He could act the fool, say something cute and meaningless, but…that wasn't the right kind of smile. Not amusement. Happiness. He wanted her to smile at him because being there with him made her happy, everything else aside.

"Of course. Sorry." She reached toward Tom, and a small flat handbag of some kind was passed to her, but as she began moving toward Liam it was a conscious effort to square the knowledge that this was Grace with the Gracie he knew.

She'd always been the girl next door. Pretty. Wholesome. Quietly unattainable. And he'd always wished he could attain her. Even during the time that he'd done his best to put her from his mind and had got on with living, anytime he'd seen that shade of sun-kissed light brown hair he'd thought of her. Every time he'd spoken to his best friend he'd thought of her, even if just to remind himself not to ask about her. He'd told himself she'd never fit into his world…but the truth was something else entirely. He was the misshapen one here.

But in that dress she was the best of Old Hollywood—flowing lines and glittering, silken elegance.

Her light brown wavy tresses had been braided somehow around her head, so the blonde highlights stood out. A style she could wear to the beach or on a picnic… He could imagine her poking daisies into the woven crown. More sweetness, and at odds with the gown and the glittering jewelry, but somehow on Grace it worked. This was how Grace would fit into his world, taking the best parts from both.

As she got closer, he felt an overwhelming desire to straighten. Stand taller. Say something to let her know, make sure she knew… If this were a movie, a writer would have given him a great line, something that would let her know just how gorgeous she was.

"You look…" He paused, completely at a loss. Oh, was he in so much trouble…

"Do my scars show?"

"Scars?" The word fit nowhere in his mind right now. "What scars?"

She held up one of her arms and turned it so that he could see the inside.

The pain in his ankle faded as he stepped forward, tucking the cane under his arm, and reached for her elbow so he could angle her toward the light better.

A blast of cold shot into his chest as his eyes found what she referred to. A thin puckered line led from the inside of her arm back, around her triceps.

Suddenly, his hands were the ones shaking. It had come from a large injury of some kind, or had it been a surgery? Something big enough he should've damned well known. "What the hell is that from?"

"You're going to get makeup on your hands. I don't want you to have tan handprints on your tux. Believe me, makeup stands out on black material about as badly as it does on white."

"It won't smudge," Tom said from behind her, inter- rupting Liam's questioning.

And she'd said scars. Not scar. "There are more?"

"Other arm too, but the rest are covered. Dress…"

More? He peeled his hands off her before he lost con- trol, and took a step backward, still not using the cane but putting her outside of the reach of his hands so he didn't shake her until she answered him.

"What happened? What happened to give you scars?"

"They're from my accident."

"What accident?"

The elevator doors opened with a ding and Miles interrupted them. "The car is here, Liam. If we don't go down now, it's going to cut into your carpet time."

Confusion flashed in her eyes, and behind it regret. He didn't know about her accident. She might as well have said the words for how clearly he could read it in her expression. Another reminder of their time apart. Or was it memories of this accident when he hadn't come to visit her as she'd recovered?

Stepping toward him, she pulled his cane from under his arm and put it into the appropriate hand. "We'll talk about it later. Don't want to be late, right? We'd better go before you have to do something sensible like spend less time walking on your injured ankle."

A moment later the elevator whisked them downward, leaving him with too many questions to think about. But she was right. If they didn't go now, he'd have to move faster than his ankle would appreciate. Something else to talk about at dinner.

"Do I match you?"

"Match?"

He shuffled a little back so he could see her again.

"Like complement? Does my dress complement your tux? It's got kind of an old-fashioned cut..."

"It's made to look like something from the era." He confirmed the cut of his tux, but the nervous light that had replaced the regret in her eyes made him add, "I think it does, but really anything complements a black tie." Her nervousness redirected his teeth-gritting focus. "Besides, I'm pretty sure I'm the one complementing you tonight."

"No," she said, reaching up to smooth his jacket at the shoulders and down the sleeves. "That's silly. You're the star of the movie, which I'm looking forward to seeing." She stopped smoothing, her hand resting on his chest where she'd fluffed the silk kerchief in his pocket. "Are you sure you're up to this?"

Fretting. Fussing. Focusing attention away from herself. Away from the scars...which he hadn't even assured her barely showed. Later. He couldn't bring them up again right now.

"I'm up to it." He'd keep her hand resting on his chest all evening, keep her there in that small space in front of him, looking up in that way that made him feel...something he didn't want to feel. Possessive. And destructive.

But he recognized his chance to start evening things

out between them. "Even if I wasn't up to it, I'd be up to it...just to have you on my arm tonight."

For a moment the worry disappeared from her eyes, a kind of wonder replacing it.

Those were good words. Maybe not the perfect thing to say but it was close.

He shifted her hand from his chest to his elbow as the elevator stopped and opened on the ground floor, then planted the cane and used it to lead her out.

As they walked, she was still looking up at him, the wonder turning to shock. They passed through the lobby of red marble and dark walnut, and when they made it to the car she still looked shocked. He lifted a finger to her chin. "You're beautiful, Grace."

The urge to kiss her nearly overwhelmed him. If she were his, he would've.

Instead, he closed her mouth and let his hand fall to the small of her back to steer her into the car.

Did no one ever tell this golden angel how magnificent she was?

God help him, he was in so much trouble.

CHAPTER SIX

ON THE FLIGHT down to Virginia, Grace once more had Liam with his foot propped up, shoe off and a cold pack placed over those injured ligaments.

It seemed she'd no sooner settled herself in her dress than they were out of the plane and in a limo.

It all happened so fast. They stopped at the curb-side where the carpet started, and when Liam had his cane in position and her on his other arm, he moved her forward.

People, screaming and cheering, lined both sides. Flashes came from all directions. A quaint refurbished theater with gilded fixtures on tall, heavy doors awaited them after a blessedly short carpet walk. Liam shook hands as they went, posed for pictures, took a couple selfies with a fan, then a number of group selfies with cameras Grace funneled toward him and then back to the crowd.

And then they were inside the theater, a manager leading them through to a back exit where the limo waited.

Grace couldn't swear she'd even taken a single breath before it was all over and they were back at the airport, with her once more settling a cold pack on his ankle.

"You all right?" Liam asked.

When she looked at him, he nodded to the seat beside him. "They want us buckled in so we can get back into the air."

"Right. Right…" She gathered her dress as best she could to prevent wrinkling, and sat down.

"You look shell-shocked, Gracie. Want something to drink?"

"No. I'm fine. I just… That was… A lot."

"Not to scare you but that was small. The next one will be much bigger. But it was overwhelming to you because it was your first. That's over. You've done it now, and we won't be in such a rush to get through the next one. Just lean back and breathe."

Breathe. She didn't really have anything to do but make sure Liam didn't walk all over the place. And she was very good at walking.

"Do you always go from one right to another one?" Grace asked Liam, sitting by the door in the back of the limo as it spirited them through crowded evening streets toward the New York theater.

"It's not unheard of, but not usually. We were on location in Virginia for three months, and the film was based on a book written by a local author, who's like a hometown hero to them. So that's why it was scheduled."

"I get that," she said, "But why have two on one day?"

"Sometimes they hold the theater launch back until after the premiere. Though it's pretty common to have more than one, and they don't want to hold the film any longer than necessary. It's all decided by the marketing people for best impact. I just go where they tell me."

He scooted a little closer and wrapped his arm around her shoulders, pulling her against him. "You thought it was all fancy parties where everyone stood around telling each other how amazing they looked, and drinking too much."

"Actually, I thought you all got dressed up, but then behaved like it was a frat party, with gobs of public nudity and body shots," she filled in, grinning at him. His heat felt good at her side. It was still summer, and the Virginia carpet had been hot, but the air-conditioning on both the jet and in the cars had been high enough to chill her.

Liam looked at her, the fondness in his eyes cutting through some of the chill too. Enough that she didn't know how to respond again. He'd done that to her earlier too, when he'd said she was beautiful.

"Why are you looking like that?" she asked, needing him to stop before he confused her again.

Not that he stopped, he just smiled too. "Because you finally smiled."

"Didn't I smile enough in Virginia?"

"You did. But you weren't smiling at me until now."

She felt her cheeks going pink and forced herself to look down. He'd said she was beautiful earlier, and now he'd looked at her like she was sunshine. In one day. What her earlier self would've given to hear those sweet words from him.

Even so, she couldn't keep the smile from her face right now, though she tried to edge back to the earlier subject. "My real mental image was that it was all about the after-party with champagne and wild behavior. If it is, I'd like you to keep that from me. I much prefer this, even if I'm really tired of posing for pictures."

He let her get back to it without doing anything else that might make her emotions go haywire. "We're skipping the after-party."

"Oh, thank God." That would be less time in the dress and less time with him on that foot.

"This time it will start the second we step out of the car. Hope your cheeks aren't too sore from the last round."

Half a block in front of them crowds had gathered, and police stood in front of barricades, directing traffic—regular traffic in one direction, and them another.

They'd just done this a couple hours ago, but he'd been sitting still since then. And when you did that with an injury... "Remember to use the cane more when you first put your weight on the leg. It's been resting for a while, so that pain is going to scream through your leg when you first—"

"I know. I've figured that part out." His hand moved to cup her bare shoulder, the pad of his thumb stroking the front curve.

The car stopped and her stomach lurched with it.

"You've already done this once," he said, obviously picking up on her discomfort. "You're the belle of the ball, Grace. Just remember to smile."

The door opened and she had to make herself move. "I'm the belle of the ball," she whispered to herself as she accepted a hand out from the man who'd opened the door. "Thank you." She stepped to the side, reminding herself to smile as she made room for Liam.

As soon as his handsome head appeared above the door, so many flashes went off that as she turned to look at him and check his balance, all she could see were spots in her vision.

"I'm okay, Grace," he said, before she could ask, then slipped his hand into hers and steered her around the door so they could make the walk. "Just follow my lead. Stop when I stop. Pose and smile. Just like before.

Only with more stops this time. We'll also make a wide zig-zag path down the carpet."

"How many zigs?" She stopped when he did and turned slightly toward him, her heel butting against the center of the other foot, just like Tom had told her to stand.

Pause. Smile. Walk.

"I don't know. Ten."

"Two," she countered. "The more you zig, the more you walk. You said I was here to keep you from having to walk too much. Otherwise why am I wearing this dress?"

"Because you're my date, and you have to wear clothes to a premiere, no matter what your freewheeling California inclinations say. Hippy."

She laughed despite herself. "Idiot." But his joking made her relax. "I'm willing to up to four zigs. Any more than that and I'm going to take your cane and start clubbing your fans so that they stay back."

"Five."

They were moving again slowly, with him waving, as they headed for the first point of the zig.

"Fine, but only because an odd number would flow better toward the door with you going in this direction first." She quieted down as he approached the edge.

Once again, pieces of paper, magazines, pictures… things were thrust at Liam, and he dutifully signed and shook hands.

Every time he was ready to walk again she joined him and they made their way back to the other side, pausing for photos along the way, and once to speak with a camera crew who called to him for an interview.

Why was he using a cane?

Who was his date?

Was she the reason he'd broken up with Simone Andre?

Though she saw a tic in his jaw with the last question, Liam answered everything politely. Sprained ankle. Grace Watson. No. He'd begged Grace to come with him last night, and she'd miraculously been available.

At the last leg of the carpet, a very little boy at the front asked about the cane. Even though Liam had given this answer at least thirty times since that first crew had asked, he stopped in front of the boy and shifted his weight to the good leg so he could pinch the pants leg and lift it, showing the expanse of white tape poking up above his sock. "I fell down when I was running."

"Does it hurt?"

"Oh, it hurts, but I wanted to come and have fun here tonight with everyone. Plus, they gave me a cane to use and it's got a sword in it." He pulled the handle up to give the boy a peek of the blade. "I couldn't pass up a chance to use a sword cane."

And he actually had been using the cane, and not just as a cool prop. Why he'd ever been upset to begin with still didn't compute with her.

There was some gasping over the awesome sword cane, the boy lifting his own pants leg to show Liam his bandaged knee.

As much as she wanted to usher him right off into the theater and make him sit, make him take the weight off it, there was no way she'd interrupt wound comparisons and "I fell too" stories.

By the time she thought her face would split from smiling, the little guy's mother opened her bag and after some digging produced and unwrapped a colorful bandage.

She watched as Liam lifted his cuff and the little boy crawled beneath the velvet rope to pull Liam's sock down and place the bandage right over the bump of his taped ankle, a cartoon character bandage in an expanse of white tape.

Her heart squeezed as she watched. He might complain about how crowds drained him, but he loved it too. He was so sweet to the boy she had to look away briefly to banish sappy tears.

He fought to be at all these events, and it wasn't just because he wanted his career to continue being wildly successful—although, of course, that had to factor in. It was something more.

He posed for pictures with the boy this time, and their matching bandages, then made it the last few steps into the theater.

"Let's find where we're sitting. I need to sit."

"Of course you do. It still took forty-five minutes to make it into the building."

"And that was fast, Grace. I've spent two hours out there before." He leaned on the cane heavily and gestured for an usher. Soon they were being led to a small balcony to sit down. "Will we have people here with us?"

He nodded and then proceeded to name names—all of which she'd heard before, and none of whom she'd met.

Before they got there, she leaned forward in her seat to look at his leg. The tape looked tight but not tight enough to cut off circulation. She pulled the sock up for him, and set it all to rights. "Will there be any empty seats?"

He did a quick seat count and then shook his head. "Probably not."

"Can we get a footstool brought up?"

"Oh, that we might be able to do," he said, and then looked at her long enough to demand her attention. "You're always concerned about my leg and pain level."

"Of course I am."

"Because you know how it is to have an injury?"

There was an edge to his voice, prompting her to make eye contact again in the low light of the theater.

"I'd like to think that I'd still care without that painful time in my past."

"How did you get hurt?" He didn't sound angry, as he had in the hotel, but there was more emotion in his voice than she'd expect from someone who'd stayed away so effectively. And who hadn't felt the same way about her as she'd felt about him.

Even if she'd avoided asking about Liam, she'd always thought he'd probably still kept up with her through Nick. Nick was a talker, and he had spent a lot of time in the hospital with her while she'd recovered. "Nick really didn't tell you about my accident? I thought you two told one another everything."

"No. He never did. Which is pretty weird…"

Yes. Weird. Unless Nick knew about them. "I had a motorcycle accident when I was nineteen."

"I never heard about you having a motorcycle either."

"I didn't. My boyfriend at the time… It was his motorcycle. After that, I had a lot of rehab. But it pretty much scratched professional swimmer off my career list. So I'm doing the next best thing."

He made some sound of affirmation, but it didn't sound settled.

Liam leaving had made her reckless, always seeking out the bad boy. That particular bad boy had made her go to the other extreme. Which made this premiere business so out of character for her that it could've been a joke. If someone had said to her last week that she'd be glittering from head to toe at a New York City premiere she'd have definitely thought it was some kind of joke where her dullness was the punch line. Because her life had been dull, probably. Other people would find the clientele exciting, and sometimes she did, but it was hard to be impressed by celebrities when she'd known Liam as long as she had. He was a real person, and that made them all too real and flawed as well.

Maybe they were all wounded too. Maybe it took that kind of hurt to get someone from talented to artist.

"I'm going to go find the usher," she said, mostly because she didn't know what else to say. "See if we can get that footstool."

Before her musings moved onto lamentations of what she couldn't have.

"The movie was good," Grace said, shifting in the back seat of the limo, not sure of where or even how to sit now that their charade of a date was over. "You were good. Not that I expected anything different. But all those period costumes, I loved it. It felt like a real story. Not just all the flash-bang stuff that goes on in your action movies."

For the entire evening she'd been pretty much plastered to Liam's side, and now, sitting with space around her, she felt cold. And lonely. Making useless small talk also felt awkward.

"Grace Watson, are you saying you don't like my action movies?" Unlike earlier, Liam had taken a spot up by the door, his legs stretched out in front of him.

"Still playful, that's good. I guess your ankle isn't hurting as much as last night?"

"You did not answer the question but you're correct, it's not hurting as badly as last night."

She crossed her arms and lifted her brows, giving him her best told-you-so expression.

Liam crossed his arms in response. "You want me to say it?"

"I do. It's a personal failing, I know, but yes. Yes, I want you to say it." She knew she looked smug, that was the whole point of the told-you-so expression.

"You were right. I should have listened to you all along, but then I would never have gotten to have the prettiest date tonight."

She snorted. The first couple of times he'd said it she'd been too dazed to really process the words.

"You know, the more you say it, the less I believe it." They passed a building she hadn't seen on the way to the theater and she stopped to get a good look at the direction in which they were traveling. "This isn't the way to the hotel. Are we going to the airport or something?"

"No, we're going to dinner."

"You want me to be right some more? You need that thing up and iced—it's been hours."

"I need to eat too if I'm going to take one of those blessed pain-reducers, don't I?"

"Yes, and it's called room service."

"I don't want room service. I want to eat at my favorite restaurant in New York, with my date."

She didn't say anything. Arguing with the man had done no good in anything they'd butted heads over so far. He'd only agreed to the cane after he'd proved her case for her. "How about we get it to go?"

"No. We're going to go in, sit at the quiet booth I've reserved, and if you want me to I will sling my leg up in the bench beside me to have it elevated. We can eat good food and relax with no responsibilities hanging over our heads. No one asking for interviews, or pictures. Have a little wine. Can I have wine with those pills?"

"No. I know I say that a lot, but you always want a little bit more, don't you? I want to go to dinner. I want to eat where I want to eat. I want to have pain pills and wine." She shook her head, but the tension she'd been feeling had already started to drain away. Probably had started the moment that he'd agreed to use the cane. It made it easier to tease him back. "How did you stay alive this long? Luck? Your looks?"

"Yep." He reached over, wiggled an arm behind her around her waist, and slid her over to him. "Fate lets me get by with stuff because I'm too pretty to smite."

She laughed even though she knew it just egged the fool on. "So that's why Fate sent me. I'm immune to your prettiness."

The car rolled to a stop and the doorman came to open their door. "You just adore me for my winning personality? Or is it my body? I feel so cheap."

And yet he grabbed his cane and got out of the car, stepped to the side and offered her a hand.

"This is not a date," she said, taking the offered hand if for no other reason than civility—even if she was currently ignoring the fact that navigating car doors in this dress wasn't really in her usual skill set. "And no wine. Or I'm going to whine."

"Fine, fine. No wine. But I'm eating red meat and you can't stop me." He passed her hand through the crook of his elbow and led the way inside. "I come here whenever I'm in New York, they have a couple of great private booths. And if you want, I'm sure they'll even bring out a bag of crushed ice. Which I will use, in the interests of making my date happy."

"This is not a date." Grace repeated herself, this time more quietly as they wandered through the restaurant to the promised private back corner booth.

"Okay," he whispered back. "In the interests of making happy the lovely creature who went to the movies with me, and who is now going to eat with me, I will ask for ice."

They stopped at the booth and Liam sat on the side that would allow him to kick his leg up on the seat like the heathen he'd better well be if he wanted her to eat dinner with him.

Grace took the other side, and resisted the urge to ask for the ice. He'd said he would do it.

Knowing better than to test her on this—or at least she liked to think that was the reason—he dragged his foot up onto the seat and winked at her.

Menus were place before them and a bottle of the vintage Liam preferred presented to him. "No wine tonight. Water. Iced tea maybe?" He looked at Grace.

"Just water for me." She looked at the menu, but the prospect of reading words seemed too much for her. "My feminist core is shrieking, but I don't want to order. Can I just have whatever you're having? I don't think I have any room in my head to make any decisions right now."

"It's harder than it seems, eh?" he asked.

"The stop and pose, stop and smile, stop and shake hands, stop and sign things, stop and chitchat route to the movie?"

"It was better tonight. It's always better with someone there but, you know, as much as we've avoided one another for the past several years, it's been really great to have you here, Grace. I hope that's all right for me to say."

She smiled, looking down as she did so, and nodded. "You too. When you're not being infuriating. I forgot how much of a playful charmer you can be. All I've really seen is Actor Man, he of the thousand faces, since... You know."

She cut that thought off sharply, and scrambled for something else to say. She wouldn't bring that subject up now. Their forty-eight hours together were almost done. From tomorrow on they could see one another once a day, she'd go back to her less glittery existence, and he'd stay out in the limelight, adored by millions.

"The little boy..."

"Brody." He said the name she'd missed.

"You asked his name?"

"He offered it. Brody, the budding physical therapist." He lifted his pants leg and showed off the colorful bandage still plastered to his taped ankle.

"You were really great with him. As much as you say that this stuff drains you, it doesn't show. It didn't show. It only showed last night because of the limping, I think, otherwise no one would've known."

"I like kids. I don't really remember ever being that age. I mean, I remember being in kindergarten and, you know, young grades, but my life was..."

Bad. She knew his childhood had been really hard. She had always known that his mother had died from an overdose, but she just didn't know any real details. Before he'd told her about the book. That had cleared up all her confusion in a way that gave absolutely no other details. It had hurt him to even tell her that much, and it had hurt to hear it. She didn't want him to have to go through anything else like that tonight.

"Complicated," she offered quickly, giving him an

out in case he, too, wanted to avoid dissecting painful memories.

If she had her way, she'd know every single part of him, from his past, to the way he thought, to all his future plans... But it really wasn't her right to ask any probing personal questions. No matter how nice they both agreed it had been to be around each other again, he wasn't going to be around that long. Once he was back on his feet, her usefulness would be at an end.

"Complicated." Liam echoed the word. His childhood wasn't high on his list of things to talk about tonight. The waiter arrived and he tried to think of the least drippy foods to order, and shifted conversation on.

His list of things to talk about really only had two items: that night and that trench coat.

But that felt like an after-dinner conversation. So he steered them back toward small talk, safe and focused on subjects that would make her feel comfortable.

Memories they'd shared after Liam had been placed in foster care near the Watsons' home, and how he'd befriended Nick.

How she'd ended up at The Hollywood Hills Clinic.

Why she'd left professional sports.

Things he'd never let himself know about her, even when he'd wanted to know.

"I saw you once at a game," he said, as their dinner plates were taken away. "You were working on one of the players' knees. You want dessert? I want dessert."

The dessert he wanted definitely wasn't on the menu, but in the interest of sublimating his carnal desires...

"I don't think I need one."

"Split one. They have this chocolate cake thing with fruit that's really good." He ordered one and then took the ice off his ankle, sat up straighter, and slid toward her in the booth.

"If you don't want to eat it, just take one bite and I'll pretend we split it equally."

"I could move over there to you so you could keep your foot elevated."

"It's okay. We're not going to be here much longer anyway. And I think that those pain tablets are kicking in."

With a nod, Grace went about clearing a spot between them, shifting water bottles and cutlery as needed. Keeping busy.

"Grace, I need to talk about—"

Before he even got the words out her perennially straight posture went rigid, and beneath that California glow he could see her cheeks pinking up.

She still didn't want to talk about it.

"It's not what you think." He caught her hand before she could tidy any more and dragged it to his lap in the hopes that her attention followed.

"Oh, I'm sure it is."

"The thing is—and this is pretty selfish of me—I need things to be good between us. And be honest. You don't really owe it to me to listen to my explanations…"

"You really have nothing to explain." This time, catching her hand didn't settle her down and her voice rose a little as she looked everywhere but at him. "I don't blame you. I'm not mad. It was all my fault. You didn't do anything wrong. I put you into an unwinnable situation because I was young and stupid. Inexperienced in reading people's intentions…"

"Grace?"

"You've become really good at it, not that I blame you. How else are you going to keep out of those kinds of situations, especially now that you're on the Freebie List of at least seventy percent of the married women in North America, and probably a significant number of women abroad?"

"Stop."

"Barring sexual preferences, of course. Oh, then probably men too. I just couldn't even ballpark a figure on that one."

"Grace, I wanted you," he blurted out, his heart suddenly thundering in his ears, and his confession probably carried halfway across the restaurant. The waiter arrived right then and wordlessly placed the plate between them, then placed the silverware and left.

Grace rolled the hand that he held, not pulling away but as if she couldn't dispel the tension in her body unless she moved something.

"Take a bite of this thing. Strawberry. Chocolate brownie thing. Cream. Get all of it. One big bite." He kept her hand, and she still didn't pull away, but she also didn't look at him, focusing heavily on the dessert instead.

"I'm eating more than one bite of that," she finally said, and when he let go of her hand, she reached for her spoon.

"You don't have anything to say about my declaration?"

She glanced up, an uneasy smile on her face now. One of her hands slipped up to cover her collarbone protectively, then gave it a little rub. "You mean besides *I don't believe you*?"

"You think I'd yell that in a crowded restaurant if it was a lie?"

"I think…you're trying to make things right." She chose her words slowly and carefully, he could see, but the self-comforting actions had already started. "And I appreciate that, but you don't have to."

He reached over and pulled her hand from her chest, once more holding it in his own as the other fiddled listlessly with her spoon.

"What are you doing?"

"Comforting you," he murmured. "You covered your jugular notch, it's a self-comforting technique. Women often do that when they're feeling unsettled or emotionally unsafe, while men usually rub the back of the neck... There are other things that could be called tells. Like when you got out of the pool and you saw me there, your feet were pointed toward the closest door, and I knew you wanted to run."

"I wanted to go to the locker room and get dressed. And please don't do that," she muttered, bouncing the spoon in her fingers, having yet to use it for anything useful.

"Don't hold your hand?"

"Don't tell me what I'm feeling based on what my extremities are doing!"

"Fine. How about I tell you this instead: I wanted to drag you into that apartment, tear off every scrap of black lace, and make sure that you could *never* forget me. That's the truth." It was still the truth, but not one he was going to admit. He still wanted her in a way that defied logic, in a way he still had to fight his way through even when she was quarreling with him. "But because I couldn't have what I wanted—which was you, in case you're not paying good enough attention—I tried to forget it. To forget you. But I never didn't want you, Grace. You didn't read me wrong."

The spoon she bounced on her finger slipped and clattered off the table and onto the floor. She didn't reach for it; instead, she finally looked him in the eyes again, the kind of measuring look that at least said he had her complete attention. She was trying to decide what she thought.

"You were off-limits. I wasn't kidding when I said that your home and family were my safe place." She *had* to believe him. These confessions weren't easy, and if they were for nothing? "Or how much you all meant to me. Nick is my best friend, I love your family like my own. More than my own. They never measured up when they were around. It wasn't a rejection, I just didn't know how to do it right. You weren't the only one who was young and stupid. I may be older, but I'm definitely not the smarter of the two of us."

His heart beat so hard his lungs felt battered.

"There was a girl at the apartment with you. I only realized it as I was running off and I heard her call out to you."

"That girl?" He stopped, trying to recall who it was. Yes, there had been a girl… "You're going to call me a pig, but I actually can't remember her name. I sent her home right after you left." He let go of her hand and retrieved his own spoon. Once he'd got some dessert on it, he held the spoon to her lips to distract her.

Her lips parted and she leaned forward, taking his spoon into her mouth, her warm brown eyes never leaving his. He could feel the slow seductive movement of her tongue across the bowl of the spoon before he slid it back through her closed lips. Good God, he was getting too wrapped up in the idea that this was a date. His heart sped up for an entirely different reason.

"She wasn't the girl I wanted that night." His voice went hoarse and he had to clear his throat to add, "So I sent her away, and spent a long, miserable night, staring at the ceiling and waiting for Nick to get back from his date."

Here beside her, the goose bumps racing down her arms were impossible to miss. He ran the back of one knuckle down her arm, then shrugged out of his jacket and wrapped it around her, as much to warm her as to help his own willpower—hide that soft golden skin beckoning him. And maybe break the sudden heavy, sensual atmosphere that had descended on them. It had to go if he wanted to hold on to any scrap of his sanity.

No more feeding her or touching her. He needed to get the atmosphere back to a more playful, jovial mood. He took a bite for himself, an excuse to make himself stop gazing into her eyes. "Him getting back? Made things worse because your brother always seems to pick up screamers."

"Oh, God, I don't need those details," she said, laughing a little as she pulled the jacket around her and snuggled in, then focused back on him, latching onto what he'd said. "I didn't misread you. You wanted me?"

"I'm an idiot, but I'm not that big an idiot. Of course I did. You're..." He stopped again. "You're great." Great. Not perfect, he wouldn't say perfect. His heart felt too big for him in that moment. Enlarged. Sluggish. Sore. It all felt too big for him.

If he'd taken her up on it that night, maybe he'd be able to ignore that want now, but that wasn't Grace's style. Maybe she didn't even want him anymore the way he wanted her.

She shifted in her seat, turning more toward him. Open, inviting. Those walls were coming down. That had to be good. It was almost too much to hope that they could return to being friends.

"I spent the whole night thinking of what I wished

I could have done differently." She whispered her own confession.

"Just one night?" he asked, thankful for the opening to try and get things back on less shaky ground. "I spent considerably more time than that."

"No. Not just one night. But, well, my rewind fantasies of that night were not very, you know, good. In a sexy way. They were mostly about me dragging that girl out by the hair and keying your car."

That was easier to smile at. Like she'd ever do either of those things. "If you'd keyed that car I would've never noticed," he said, taking another bite of the dessert. "I still have it, though."

"You do not." The waiter replaced her dropped spoon, and Grace reached for it and helped herself to a bite this time.

"Yes, I do. It's at a shop that restores old cars now. They're gutting and rebuilding it. So, if you decide to key it in the future, I will notice and be very sad. So let's keep talking about how sad it is that we're both so hot and can't have one another."

"I never said I was hot."

"No, that was me. I implied it. I thought you'd be better at reading between the lines than that. Or we could talk about why your—what did you call them, rewind fantasies? Why weren't they satisfying? I'm told that fantasy me is a stallion."

She laughed then, so brightly that he instantly felt better. Like the whole of their history was being wiped clean. They could be friends, continue on in one another's lives, hang out with Nick and do whatever it was that people did when they hung out in groups. Go the movies without formal wear. Something.

"Well, that was the other thing." She sobered, shaking her head as her cheeks began to turn pink. "I wasn't... See, I had this idea that you would've been... my first time. So I didn't just make a stupid and unaccountably brave move for me, but for my experience level."

His head snapped back as her words settled and coldness washed over him.

"You were...?" He must have heard that wrong. "You were a virgin? You were coming to me because you were a virgin?"

CHAPTER SEVEN

"I HAD THIS HAZY, insubstantial fantasy heavily lacking satisfying details…about you being the first." Grace shrugged as she said it, like it meant nothing. Like that didn't make it worse.

Liam sat back, at a loss for words.

"I'm not still a virgin," she hastened to add. "I'm not still holding out for you or anything pathetic like that."

Once again, she had misinterpreted his behavior.

"No, I imagine if you were still holding out for me, you'd have been a damned sight happier to see me than you were," he muttered, his hand lifting to rub the back of his neck. "The guy you ended up with."

"Brad."

"Brad." He repeated the name, as if it weren't giving him those rewind fantasies about beating the hell out of *Brad*. "I don't want details! Just… Was he good to you?"

"I guess so. I haven't had very serious relationships. I always pick badly," she said, shrugging again.

"Stop shrugging. Was he the one with the motorcycle?" If her rebound guy had…

She nodded, mouth twisting to the side. No doubt she could tell by the tone in his voice, which he had no hope of disguising, exactly what he wanted to do to Brad.

"Did he survive?" Earlier, Liam hadn't thought to ask

about the ex-boyfriend, but now that he knew his name and that he'd hurt her after being her first…

"Yes. He had all the leathers and such. I was just in jeans and—"

"Okay! Stop. I can't know more right now. And to think I was hoping that this talk would make things better between us."

"It has," she said, putting her hand on his, so small and fragile to his eyes now. So breakable. He should've been there to protect her. He should've been there to make sure that Brad damned well knew he should give his date the damned leathers anytime he took them out on his motorcycle.

"Liam, I put you into a no-win situation. There was nothing you could've done right in that situation. Even if you'd done what I wanted, it's unlikely that things would've been good between us now. My rewind fantasies also included how later, after you'd come to your senses, you came after me. Sometimes with gifts."

He wanted to put his arm around her again and know that as long as she stayed by him he could keep her safe.

He pulled his hand free instead. "Those are normal girl fantasies."

"No, I mean quintessential boyfriend gifts. Like flowers, candy, and a kitten in one hand and a puppy in the other. Do you see what I'm getting at?"

"That you had relationship feelings." It had never just been about sex. She'd had relationship feelings, she'd wanted him to be the first. And now? It was worse, because his mind was exactly in the same place.

Hell.

"Right."

"Again, how does that make things better?"

"Because they're another example of my being irrational and sentimental. You were living away at that time. I was about to go to college at the other end of the state." She dropped her hand into her lap and once again the oversized shoulders of his jacket rose. "It's okay. I got over it. I met someone else."

"Brad."

"Brad," she repeated. "And then we broke up, and I met Austin. And then—"

"Stop. Please. I don't need your dating CV."

"Because this is not a date?" she prompted, grinning at him finally. "I feel better. I do. You shouldn't feel badly about events you had nothing to do with."

He felt badly about the event he *had* had something to do with. "If I had taken you aside and said *I want you but we can't do this*, it would have been better. Because then I could've been there to make sure Brad knew what I'd do to him if he hurt you."

"You assume that one change would have changed everything. Maybe it wouldn't have. Maybe it would've made everything worse. I know for sure what you telling me that would've done. It would have led to me upping my game."

"Grace, your game started with you at my front door in your underwear."

"No. My game started long before that, but then you went away and I got desperate. That was my big plan when you came back to visit. It was my grand gesture." She pushed the plate away and then flattened her hands against the tabletop. "I thought if I stopped beating around the bush, once you knew I wanted you, you'd be all for it. Everyone says teenage boys will have sex with any girl they find remotely attractive if offered the chance. I thought once the chance was offered, that the underwear would make you want me, and then ev-

erything would fall into place and they all lived hap-
pily ever after..."

"No reflection on your attractiveness, but that's not
how it works. At least not for me."

"I figured that out later. But my point is that if then
you had already wanted me and were just being rational? What eighteen-year-old girl do you know who
cares about being rational when feelings are in the way?
Heck, I barely care about rational now and I've suppos-
edly had six years to grow up since then."

The waiter came, the dessert between them was only
half-eaten, and he'd lost his appetite for the chocolate-
strawberry confection. "Check, please." He nodded toward the jacket and said, "My wallet is in the pocket
with the phone."

"No," Grace interjected before the waiter could get
away. "Two checks."

Because this wasn't a date.

There had been moments when it had felt date-like,
and then everything had gone pear-shaped.

The waiter looked at Liam for confirmation before
he went to split the order.

She frowned, but didn't keep on with the subject.
Instead, she slid the jacket off and handed it to him.
"Thank you for the loan of the jacket. Mind if I visit
the ladies while he sorts the checks out?"

"It's that way." He gestured and scooted back around
to his side of the booth as she departed the table.

Before he moved to LA proper to start chasing
the dream, he'd known about the boys who'd called
Grace, and the few that she had tried—and quietly suc-
ceeded—in making him jealous of. He probably owed
her for teaching him to hide that emotion, even though
the ability had abandoned him tonight.

He called his driver and had him ready the car and pull around to get them. The waiter brought the checks before Grace returned, and Liam paid both of them.

When Grace came back he stood with his cane and offered her his elbow again. "Checks?"

"Paid," he muttered, and added, "I don't want to fight about the check. The restaurant was my decision, and you're here as my employee, right? It's not a date. It's not two friends having dinner together. It was my responsibility. And I tipped him well for his trouble. Clear?"

She didn't take his elbow, but walked ahead of him through the restaurant for the door.

He'd known she'd had a crush on him when they'd still been in high school. Idiot though he may have been, he had been love-deprived enough that he'd developed a keen way of detecting it in every incarnation. And if he was honest with himself, that was probably a big part of the draw of his occupation. He'd gone from having very few he could claim who loved him to having thousands, to having millions. He'd gone from the unwanted son of dead junkies to the man on top of every producer's wish list.

He could identify a lot of emotions on sight—studying body language to improve his acting had come with other benefits. He could tell the difference between fondness of friends, adoration of fans, and when past girlfriends were getting Too Close to Love—aka Time to Break Up. He knew the difference between the way his parents had looked at him the times they hadn't been looking through him, and the way the Watsons had always looked at him—loving and always a little worried about him.

He could identify love in its many flavors.

But apparently he sucked at spotting a virgin.

Liam had claimed he'd wanted honesty and to clear the air. Obviously he hadn't thought that through.

Grace was just trying to be completely honest, because all her instincts said to lie about the whole ordeal. Protect herself. But when her instincts were the most selfish, that's when she did her best to ignore them. Do the opposite. Do the hard thing if it could help someone else.

Protect Liam. Absolve him of his guilt. Don't leave him wondering why she'd been the one to hold on to it for so long, make sure he knew this had never been his fault.

But this was apparently also wrong. Now that she'd told him, they sat in the back of the limo in silence and tension even worse than when she'd been wondering when he was going to bring up how much he hadn't wanted her.

"You're gritting your teeth," she said softly, trying to fix this before it got worse. "I'm fine, Liam. You should be fine too. You were right."

"I don't want to hear again that it was the only course of action. I know that. I still know that, but that doesn't make this better."

"Why? Are you such a caveman that you're angry that I've had boyfriends?"

"No. God, no. I'm not angry."

"Have you told your face that? I don't think your eyebrows got the memo. Did you ever notice that the angry characters in children's shows either have a unibrow or they have just really heavy, straight brows that come together in an angry way?"

"I never played a Muppet," he joked, if that tone could be called a joke.

She scooted up against him, mirroring the way he'd dragged her to him earlier, and lifted his arm so she could get under it. "See? I'm completely at ease with you now. I understand limits. I understand why you felt that way. I really do. At least now. You felt like you should be more like a brother to me, only I didn't feel that way. You—"

"Couldn't have won. Let's stop talking about it."

"You were the one who wanted to talk."

"And now I want to stop talking," he said, sharply enough that she leaned forward, out from beneath the arm she'd just wrapped around herself, and slid away from him on the seat again.

He was going to be the end of her sanity. Should she have trusted that instinct to keep hiding things? She'd not trusted them because when she had, all those years she'd been wrong.

Mr. I-Know-What-You're-Thinking-Because-of-Your-Feet would never have that problem. He studied body language, she studied bodily injuries. Not the kind of emotional injuries that might help her understand him.

And maybe that was why he was good at reading people. Maybe it wasn't just study but something he'd developed during a rough childhood.

She sank back into her spot on the seat and looked toward her window as he uttered an expletive and dragged her back to him.

This time, rather than wrap an arm around her, he twisted and grabbed her by the hips. One second she was on the seat, the next she was in his lap. "You're going to hurt your ankle!"

"Shut up, Grace." He caught her by the back of the neck and pulled her against him, his mouth immediately on hers.

His lips, soft and sweetened with the lingering taste of berries, stroked and nibbled, coaxing her mouth open within seconds.

Her arms rested against his chest, but as his tongue sought hers and the kiss deepened, the fighting from the past long minutes fled her mind. Instinctively, her arms slid around his shoulders as his went around her. Wide, hot hands pressed against the cool skin of her bare back and on down to her hip to keep her close to him.

She'd seen him kiss countless women, and had always wondered what it was like even while envying them. Even when her coping mechanism was to pretend that she didn't think anything about him at all.

It felt like a drug. Like it heightened her senses and tuned her into him so acutely that her heart changed rhythm to match his beat. She breathed his air and plowed her fingers into his hair to kiss him better, get him closer. Every kiss dragged her deeper into him.

A kiss like no other. If it was because of all his practice, she didn't care.

If it was because she'd been starved for it for so long, had imagined it so many times, she didn't care what that said about her either.

Their time together was almost at an end. Soon they'd be back at the clinic, and frequent visits would dwindle to only a few and then back to none. None, because that was normal for them. They'd done all they could to unweave all their ties six years ago, and she had no illusions that he'd start unweaving them again once he no longer had to have her with him. He might still want her, but there were so many women who could be whatever he wanted. A girlfriend without their baggage, without their obstacles, without jeopardizing the friendship he held dear.

This bubble that New York cast around them, it felt like a different planet. A place where they could talk about that stupid trench coat, and a place where inexplicable anger and hungry kisses could confirm that old desire still clung to them both. The only place it could exist.

The door they sat beside opened, a blast of humid air hitting them both. Liam jerked his head back, eyes glazed and panting.

"Sir?" the doorman said. "Want me to close the door back up?"

Tonight they were at the front entrance. She'd forgotten that they weren't sneaking in and out through the back since he'd deigned to use the cane. A flash went off. Then another. Stupid cameras.

She felt him retreat before he'd moved an inch.

The wall came up, and he put her down gently. The next instant he had his cane and had climbed from the car.

This time he didn't wait for her to get his elbow but started forward with the cane and a stronger hobble.

She got her bag and accepted a hand out from the doorman, thanking him before she went to catch up with Liam.

Something had just happened, she just wasn't sure what.

Two days later, decked out in her classy, cotton, roomy, embroidered polo and slacks, Grace walked beside her morning patient at the clinic, holding on to the small woman's support belt as she used the double bars to take shaky but supported steps toward the end.

Finally, a patient who didn't confuse her.

A patient who liked her and listened to her advice.

"You're doing great. Don't rush."

"I want to sit down and the sooner I get to the end, the sooner I get to sit down," Mrs. Peters said.

"And every step gets you closer to needing to sit less. You're doing so well. I can honestly say you're the best patient I have had in days."

The woman stopped midway and Grace kept holding on to the support belt, as she always did.

"I need just a little breather."

"Take your time. You standing here without walking is still making you do work."

"Yes, it is. I don't know how I got so weak."

Grace knew. Stroke. It had been caught fairly quickly, but it had still had time to do some damage.

"Muscle weakens really fast. Many of the people who come visit me here don't actually even have direct accidents or illnesses to blame for the atrophy. It happens if you just spend too much time sitting. My gran needed a bit of rehab after she had particularly nasty flu, just because she wasn't active in that time. It sneaks up on you."

Mrs. Peters nodded and inched her hands along the bars, supporting herself that way before they took another step. "A good reason to keep going."

"You can wait a bit more if you want to. It's probably only…six more steps to the end. That was one. Five more."

Other physical therapists on staff came and went with their patients during the day, but the facilities came with the kinds of equipment that made it possible to do this kind of work with only one therapist. She had safety harnesses and leads that hooked to the ceiling if the client was too heavy for the belt, but Grace preferred the belt. She'd liked it best when she'd been rebuilding her own muscle after her accident. It was smoother than the cables. Felt more secure, even if that was the opposite of true. Being connected to a person rather than some apparatus brought trust into the equation, and she'd swear that patients who could use the belt with her help got better faster.

Together they counted the steps, and once Mrs. Peters got to the end, Grace helped her turn and sit in the chair that she'd already placed there. "Let me get you some water. Don't go walking around while I'm gone, now."

She stepped into the storage room and snagged a cold bottle of water from the cooler. Her phone rang when she was in there. She glanced at the screen and rolled it to voice mail.

She didn't want to talk to Nick. She was having a hard enough time finding ways to not think about Liam, without Nick talking about anything. He invariably talked about his best friend.

And she was a terrible liar, and what was she supposed to say if he asked about her weekend? *Great. I went to New York and made out with your best friend who I'd currently like to strangle because he's being a big taciturn jerk?*

After the steamy kiss in the back of the limo he'd gone to his room and she to hers, and she hadn't seen him again until the morning when Miles came to knock and give her the ten-minute warning before they went to the airport and she'd gone to Liam's suite to wrap his ankle.

Yes, he'd accepted the ice.

He'd been polite but had slept most of the flight.

He'd taken the anti-inflammatories when she'd foisted them on him.

But what he'd refused to do was talk. He didn't actually say, *I don't want to talk to you.* There had been no yelling. He'd just failed to engage about anything.

"I'd like to watch television for a bit, Grace," Mrs. Peters said. "I didn't sleep well last night and feel tired today, but my son isn't coming to pick me up for another half an hour."

Grace flipped the brakes off on the chair and wheeled the small, frail woman around to a wall-mounted television above where the treadmills faced. She confirmed that Mrs. Peters wanted her to phone her son to come and pick her up.

She didn't have any other clients this afternoon as her clients had been shifted to other therapists—she'd only had Mrs. Peters because of a scheduling misunderstanding.

What she should do was call Liam and check on him. Even if he didn't want to talk to her about anything else, he was the one who had dragged her into this patient-therapist relationship, so she'd do the job she was supposed to do.

She dialed.

Liam answered on the second ring. "Afternoon, Grace."

"Hi. Just checking on the ankle. Doing all right? Keeping it elevated? Heat instead of ice?"

"Doing all prescribed actions."

She opened her mouth but heard Liam's name on the television and turned to look at it.

"You're on TV. Mrs. Peters is watching something. Interview."

"I had a couple of interviews this morning."

"Did you use your cane?"

"I did. And they came to the house so I didn't have to go to them. Foot elevated and all that. I told you I'd do what you told me as soon as I was able to."

A picture of Grace flashed up on the television, all decked out in her beautiful deep taupe, sparkly halter gown. "They asked about me?"

Watching the interview and talking to Liam at the same time was…weird.

"Is that you, Grace?" Mrs. Peters asked. "You know that Liam Carter?"

"Yes. And it's… Yes." She answered Mrs. Peters first and then added into the phone, "Why were they asking?"

She stopped when Liam's eighteen-inch head began laughing off the idea of dating her. Just his physical therapist. Just a friend from childhood. Just there to make sure he didn't do anything silly with his ankle in wraps.

"Wow," she said into the phone, not even sure what she felt about the denial. The way bighead TV Liam phrased it, the notion was laughable. Like there had been no kissing. No history worth mentioning aside from having been childhood friends. Nothing romantic at all.

"It's just the way you handle the press, right?" he said, trying to lead her to the same conclusion.

But all she could say was, "Wow."

Mrs. Peters's son arrived, having just wandered back inside from the grounds. She needed to go.

"I'll call you tomorrow to set up your first appointment in two days." Before he could say anything, she hung up and stashed her phone.

The chair her patient was currently using belonged to the facility, so she needed to transfer her back to her own chair and remove the belt once she was securely seated. She could think about Big Laughing Head Liam later.

Right now she didn't have room inside her own small head for all...that.

"What the hairy hell, Liam?"

Liam winced into his phone at his best friend's voice crackling down the line, loud and sharp enough to peel the eardrum from his ear. He'd been expecting Nick to call all afternoon, but he'd expected to get a greeting out before the expletives came into play.

It took a little effort, but he kept his voice steady and calm. He deserved his friend's wrath, but knowing that still didn't make it easier. "Hi, Nick. I guess you've been watching the gossip blogs."

"No, television, actually. And there you were with my sister in New York. Together. Holding hands, and then more... So let me ask again, what the hairy hell, Liam?"

"I sprained my ankle." Liam had expected a call, but for some reason he hadn't expected anger. Even in the rare instances that he and Nick had disagreed, it had only ever gotten physical once. And that time? His temper had started it, over nothing of consequence, and it had ended after they'd exchanged punches.

He'd always skipped this part during his Interlude with Grace fantasies. Consequences were rarely fantasy material, so he'd cut off anytime his imaginings had strayed in that direction.

"And?" Nick said.

"And I went to Grace to get help to finish my press tour and go to the premieres, she went with me to the East Coast premieres because having a date helps keep me from doing as much walking as I do when I'm alone. Right now, I'm sitting with my foot elevated and a heating thing on it. I have physical therapy at the clinic starting in a couple days. After I've had a mandatory rest on it."

"That doesn't explain the shots of her on your lap in the back of a limo, man."

No, it didn't.

That he couldn't explain. He'd done precisely what he'd sworn he'd never do—he'd crossed lines with Grace. "That was bad judgment. A mistake."

"You could have found another date. You could have found twenty dates to take with you and keep you from walking around too much."

He gripped the phone and switched to the other ear, this one starting to hurt from how hard he'd been smashing it with the earpiece.

One mistake in fifteen years wasn't so much.

Especially considering that he had turned her down in that trench coat, not that he had ever told Nick that. And he wouldn't tell him now. Nick didn't know about it and Grace deserved more. "It's complicated, but it's fine. Everything's fine now. It was a kiss, we didn't do anything else."

"Then why isn't she responding to my texts or answering my calls?"

"I don't know. Because you're acting like a possessive older brother?" The words came out before he could stop them and Liam suppressed a sigh, trying again. "She's seen the interviews I did this morning, so she's probably not answering because she didn't want to talk about it."

"Why not? What else did you do?"

"Dude! Do you really think I'd ever set out to hurt her?"

He heard Nick sigh and after a moment he said in a quieter tone, "You're my best friend so don't take this the wrong way, but Grace is not a player. She's a good girl. She went through a bad-boy phase and she couldn't handle it. I'm not sure how she grew up around us and remained an innocent little angel, but she did. She can't handle you."

Nick saw what he wanted to see, but there was a naughty side to Grace that Liam would never expose. A side that family should never see. But other than that, she pretty much fit the word Nick had selected. "I didn't molest her."

"You don't have to. All you have to do is be yourself. She's been more than half in love with you since she was twelve years old."

"She had a crush."

"No. She had…she had feelings for you. That's why when she stopped talking about you I stopped inviting her out with us. You still come up in conversations, but she shut down after you left. For a long time. I don't know what she feels now, I just know that you're a weak spot for her. You might not mean to make women fall at your feet, but it could be messy with Grace. Even if you don't mean to hurt her…"

This understanding and caring older brother thing chafed his already raw conscience, and he couldn't keep the irritation out of his voice. "Are you telling me to stay away from her?"

"Do I have to?"

"No. I'm seeing her for my physical therapy, but we're not traveling together anymore. They've got me scheduled for, like…ten visits. Five days a week for two weeks, weekends off. And it will be in a clinical setting. She's good at what she does, and she understands what's going on. She's the one who was taping my ankle and keeping me upright this weekend." He could probably find all that with a different physical therapist, and that's where his conscience was catching. The secret was out, so any decent physical therapist could see him in the clinic for the next two weeks. There were probably even other PTs at the clinic he could see instead.

But he didn't want to go to them. And that he couldn't defend, so when Nick started cautioning him again, Liam cut in. "I know you're protective, but you don't have to protect her from me. I love your family, Nick. I've got to go, but give her some space. She'll call you back when she wants to talk."

He hung up before he started shouting.

Because, yes, he'd screwed up, and he kept screwing up when it came to Grace.

When she'd called earlier with that interview playing in the background, he'd been hoping she'd walk out of the room, or that someone would change the channel. It had been an example of what not to do: go to an interview without knowing what you were going to say about everything. He hadn't known what to say about Grace, so he'd stuck with the physical therapist story they'd sold to his producers. It was easy. It flowed off the tongue. He'd had to force the levity there at the end, and the laugh had rung false to his ears. But, then, he knew his fake laughs from his real ones. He'd gotten good enough at faking them that most other people didn't. Grace hadn't spent enough time with him in the past few years to even have a chance of recognizing them.

To her ears, that all probably sounded legit.

Everything with her had somehow spiraled out of control. That dress had made him stupid. Dinner. The conversation he should have never started. A smarter man would have just left that subject alone rather than pick at it, thinking he could fix it.

He dropped the phone onto the table beside him before he gave in to the urge to throw it.

He was supposed to sit still for three whole days. All he wanted to do was run. Run from all this, find a peaceful beach and let his feet pound wet sand.

And it was the first time he'd ever wanted to run from any of the Watsons.

When he'd first known them and he'd run, it had been toward their house. The safe place. The place with parents who'd made sure he'd done his homework, given him a standing invite to dinner, and had always picked up a third one of anything they'd bought for their own two kids.

Even when she'd shown up at his door in her black underwear, he hadn't wanted to run from her. Every step away had been sluggish and hard.

He didn't want to feel that again. He just didn't know how to fix things with her. It could be that they could never be friends. That there was too much there for them to resist. Too much pull. Too much need—to laugh, to kiss, to talk.

They might never be able to be friends, and if he kept trying, the one friendship he could hold on to would sour.

Because Nick was right. Even if he didn't mean to, he would hurt Grace in the long run. She was innocent.

She was good and loyal. She had a shining example of a long, happy marriage to aspire to.

And the look in her eyes when she'd talked about the bandage exchange with little Brody. Grace was mother material. Grace was built for marriage and the fairy tale. While he was doomed to be surrounded by addicts and to watch them fall off, one by one, she had white picket fences and playdates in her future. He was the product of something twisted and ugly. He knew enough about the way people passed their sickness on to their families, their children…and he couldn't risk it.

Nick was right. He needed to stay away. He just needed to keep things cool between them until then.

Professional. Being friends would never work. Not now.

Not after that kiss.

CHAPTER EIGHT

THREE DAYS SINCE Liam had last seen Grace, he walked with the aid of his crutches into The Hollywood Hills Clinic. After signing in, he headed downstairs, praying for a good reception.

Their first day back she'd called to check on him, but he hadn't heard her voice since that call. Oh, she'd still checked in on him twice each day, which was probably more than any other physical therapist did with unruly patients, but it had been via text. Short texts. Terse texts. One-word texts: Update?

And he'd taken the hint. Don't call her. Because what could he say?

I can't kiss you anymore because your brother will be mad at me?

I can't kiss you anymore because all I want to do is rip your clothes off and find new, creative, and wildly satisfying ways to hurt my ankle?

Without direction from her, he decided to go to the big room with the equipment rather than the pool this morning.

"Morning." Her greeting came from the office area and he forced himself fully into the room.

Liam tilted an ear, rolling her words and tone around

in his mind as he called back, "Morning. Am I the first patient?"

Come out of there, Gracie. I need to see you, to see how you are...

"You're my first patient," she confirmed, stepping out of the office. "Everyone's got their first appointment of the day. You're not late, I just scheduled you about fifteen minutes after theirs." Busily tapping on the tablet she carried to make notes, she didn't even look at him.

Which told him enough. She was still very unhappy with him.

"Where are the others?"

"I don't know. There are three of us here, and a few different therapy rooms that can be used. We're going to one of the private rooms since we're starting light this morning." She gestured for him to follow her and stepped back out. A short distance away a bright corridor turned off and he followed her to the last room.

Inside there was a work table along with some chairs and counters. All very modern, clean, and comfortable looking as far as examination tables went.

What he should be aiming for was to handle this in a wholly professional capacity. It would be wonderful if they could be friends without all the rest of it, but it just didn't look likely. So feeling let down that she didn't want to look at him made him an idiot.

"Where do you want me?"

"Hop up on the table if you can," she said, putting the tablet down and grabbing a rolling stool for herself.

"Of course I can. I've been navigating stairs with these suckers for days. I'm just about to go pro in the Stair Climbing with Crutches event." He maneuvered himself up onto the table and scooted back, finally letting himself look at her more closely when he settled.

All that professional nonsense aside, part of him still wanted her to smile at him. He had to do better than this.

Back in normal clothes, back in their own corners, she looked at him much like she had that first day: like she wanted nothing to do with him.

"I'm just going to unwrap and have a look at it. Have you been having any trouble wrapping it?"

"Yes. I am not nearly as good at it." He leaned back and held his leg out for her to do whatever she was going to.

Still not looking at him, which was probably for the best. Eye contact led to words, and he had no words to offer her. Every time he tried to think about what to say, his mind invariably turned to replaying the limo ride, the way every time his tongue had slipped into her mouth she had rewarded him with moans and sighs, with pressing closer, with her hand tangling in his hair.

God. Stop it.

All he'd managed to riddle out was the fact that they'd have to go back to operating in strictly separate worlds after this ankle business was finished. If he were a stronger man—a better man—he could control himself. But apparently he couldn't do that.

His foot bare, she stashed the support implements to the side and gently turned his leg this way and that to examine it.

And there would be no wincing. He might not be strong in mind but he would be…strong in pain control.

"How does it look?"

"A little better. The bruising where the blood pooled isn't much different, but it's almost gone from the higher areas, away from where the actual damage occurred. But we really can't push it today. We're going to measure range of motion, what you can do on your own without my help, and what you can do with a little help from me. Did you take any pain medicine this morning?"

"I took the one you have to eat with. It helps more than the other."

She nodded and got some kind of protractor and a chair and began walking him through basic movements.

Businesslike, but still gentle with touches.

His range of motion was really bad. She had him moving until it hurt, and she would gently press until he cried uncle.

The up-and-down motion, the usual walking foot motion, was better than he'd thought it would be but any rotation in the socket made him want to jerk his leg out of her hands.

She got him down from the table and into one of the recliners.

"Want my foot up?"

"Not yet. We're going to do a paraffin bath first."

"Wax?"

"Yep, hot wax. It's not as hot as drippy candle wax because it melts at a lower temperature, but it is like no heat you can apply at home. It'll feel..." She stopped when her phone rang and she fished it from her thigh pocket. A quick scan and she gave the barest shake of her head and swiped it out. "What was I saying?"

"I think you were saying the hot wax was going to feel good."

"Better than good, really. We'll dip, I'll wrap your leg in hot towels and let you sit in it for about twenty minutes, and then we'll measure again."

The phone buzzed.

She grabbed it again and glanced at the screen. Then

turned the thing off completely and dropped it on the counter. The expression on her face…well, it was exactly the expression he'd imagined on her face every time she'd sent her one-word texts the past couple of days.

"Something wrong?"

"My brother is hounding me." She knelt and rolled up his pants leg. "We'll do this every day before we get going so you might want to wear shorts in here. Just an idea. No one to impress. No danger of it getting on your slacks."

"Okay." He looked at the phone and then at her stiff shoulders. He shouldn't ask, but it wasn't about kissing. Not exactly. Only kind of. And about the fact that his best friend thought he was a louse. Think about that. Focus on the consequences. "He's been upset with me."

"Yeah, I worked that out our first day back."

She didn't ask. Did that mean she didn't want to know how that had been going? With the way she was ignoring texts, he had to wonder what Nick had said to her.

"Both of those were him?"

"Yes. I'm not speaking to him right now."

"Why not?"

She settled the cuff above his knee and wheeled the paraffin thing over to him, but stood and retrieved towels he could only guess were hot before she guided his foot up and into the bath.

"Is he telling you to stay away from me?"

"Is that what he's telling you?"

"Pretty much," he muttered. "I told him you were helping me."

"Yep. That's what the physical therapist is supposed to do."

Zing.

She submerged his leg to mid-calf in the deep bath, and though it was plenty hot she didn't leave him soaking, just shook out one towel and as soon as his leg was out she wrapped the towel around it. And then another, and another.

Soon she had it completely encased, and nodded at the lever on the side of the chair. "Put the foot up now. I'm going to put you on a twenty-minute timer, and then we'll get you out of it."

"Is it going to turn hard?"

"Somewhat."

"So how do we…get out of it without causing pain after it gets hard?"

Grace stood up and went to wheel the bath away from him. Something she'd been asking herself for days. *How do we get out of this without causing pain?*

He had been referring to the wax, presumably, but it didn't feel that way. They'd now resorted to talking in code, because no one could say what they really meant. Which was just…great.

"It'll feel good for a while." The whole while, without a doubt. "You probably won't want to come out of it by the time it's done." That she was less certain of, at least if they were talking in code. If he was just talking about the wax, her problems were actually far less significant than she figured them to be. He got much less sexy if she also made him an idiot in her mind.

"I don't doubt that at all," he said, his words so quiet she might have missed them if she weren't so primed and tuned in to him.

Definitely talking in code.

She rolled her stool back, needing to make the room

a little bigger…because all she really wanted to do was stand up and beg him to kiss her again. "I suppose it's about risks. What you're afraid of and what you're willing to risk."

Risks. She shouldn't be the one who had to take all the risks. Was that what this would require? It hadn't seemed that way in the limo because that had been Liam's doing. For once. He'd been the one reaching for her. And then he'd laughed off the very idea of them being together. She couldn't even wish he wasn't so close to her family, because she knew now exactly how much his time with them had meant to him, and how it had probably saved his life.

"Well, you shaved my leg before, so that should help."

Was he still talking in code?

"Right. Not going to rip hair out." She twisted to snatch her phone off the counter and turned it on, checked texts and messages, then stashed it in her pocket. "I'll be careful, Liam. I have no desire to hurt you."

"Me either," he said, both hands lifting to rub over his face.

"You want me to leave you alone to soak in it?"

He dropped his hands heavily in his lap, finally looking her in the eye.

She saw regret there, matching what his voice told her. But Grace knew how terrible her instincts were with regard to this man. "All right."

A quick detour and she retrieved a remote control to give to him, pointing out a sticker on the back with the Wi-Fi password on it. "For your amusement in the meanwhile. I'll be back in twenty, and we'll roll the wax off and check your range of motion, then go through the exercises you're to do today and tomorrow. I don't need to see you tomorrow, but I will check in. And you can call if you have trouble. It's only a few gentle exercises today and tomorrow, mostly just about keeping the joint working without interfering with the healing. I'll go over the instructions when I get back. And bring in a package prepared for you to take with you with a moist heat pack and sheet with exercises in little pictures."

Liam took what she handed him and let it drop to his lap. "Thanks, Grace. I...I owe you."

"No, you don't. You pay me to do this, just like all the double time you're being billed for travel and round-the-clock care."

She wanted more, she knew that now, but she had absolutely no idea how to go about turning this mess into something more. Or even if she should try. The only thing she knew she had to do was try to keep things going, get through this, and see what happened.

That's what she always did.

Since her accident the only risks she'd taken had been with regard to Liam. All the rest of her life was Safety First. But in his presence? She kept throwing caution to the wind. Which should probably tell her something.

She stepped out of the room, set the timer on her phone, and headed back to the office. If he was going to be in therapy for the next two weeks, she should probably invest in some kind of wall padding or helmet for all the beating her head against the wall she'd no doubt be doing.

Once in the office, she closed the door and called her brother back.

She loved Nick. She really did. She knew he wanted

the best for her, and he probably felt compelled to protect her.

But she was a big girl, and it was past time he figured that out.

Grace had RSVP'd Freya Rothsberg and Zack Carlton's wedding weeks ago. She even had a dress and new strappy sandals picked out. What she didn't have was a date.

Today she'd begun to feel the pressure of that. She'd blame Liam. How in the world was she supposed to find a date for a wedding when she had movie stars in her eyes?

The problem with having stupid squishy feelings for a celebrity patient was not just knowing that she shouldn't—ethics got involved because he was her patient. She could hold out and feign something professional for the few hours a week that they spent on his rehab, which should have made things easier, but it hadn't.

But the ethics mattered to the clinic, even in their case where their history was so deep and complicated that it made the ethics question reach new depths of murkiness.

This morning's early visit would involve time in the water to get him walking in a near-weightless environment.

Which meant it was time for her to change into her bathing suit.

Normally, she'd use the one-piece that came with shorts and really concealed her assets. But due to a series of phone meetings today Liam was coming in a good two hours before they usually started seeing patients.

And she was going to make the most out of that situation because, murky ethics or not, she did want more from him. She just had to start laying the groundwork now even if she couldn't act on it while he was her patient, and also because her grand gestures to seduce the man had never seemed to work out the way she'd envisioned.

She was going to wear her black bikini, the one she kept for swimming when no one else was in the pool. The one she'd been wearing that first day when he'd stumbled over her.

Because in the four days since she'd seen him, Grace had come to some realizations.

She could deal with humiliation, but she couldn't handle not knowing what it would be like to be with him.

Liam got under her skin more than anyone ever had, and if that never happened again, she'd regret not experiencing it.

Yes, anything to do with him made her completely unable to predict how it was going to go—she couldn't make a safe play because she didn't know what was safe when it came to Liam. Not trying and going another five, or fifteen, or fifty years wondering what if? Or living with the humiliation she'd become so accustomed to if he turned her down?

Knowing he wanted her made that at least easier to stomach.

It wasn't a great plan, but she'd lived a safe life too long. She needed some risk. Liam wouldn't be the death of her, and if she was lucky, it would give her the kind of symmetry that her heart needed. Finish something that had started back then.

She went to change.

And if this bikini didn't work, that was okay: it was stage one. She had something much flimsier to try if she had to break out bigger ammunition for stage two.

Maybe she should convince him to go for a house call. His pool or the one at her place. There were pools to be had in LA where she could lure him with privacy and tempt him with tiny bikinis.

Not a great plan, but it was better than the trench coat. At least in theory.

"This exercise is not as advertised," Liam said, sliding into the hotel's rooftop pool he'd rented for the evening and had closed an hour early for his therapy with Grace, watching her across the pool where she stood in a black bikini so small only microkini enthusiasts would say it wasn't revealing enough.

The woman's bathing suits just kept getting smaller.

She dropped the towels she'd been carrying at the edge and slid into the water.

"It's water. We're going to be walking and swimming tonight, working the joint in three different ways."

"And we could have done this at the clinic. I know what you're up to, Watson."

Driving me crazy.

The use of her last name got her attention and Grace swam to his side of the pool, no doubt because it was faster than walking, even though the water wasn't more than waist deep on him. She stopped and stood in front of him, the water sluicing down her body, rippling over that soft, golden skin. He sighed and leaned back against the side.

True to her guarantees, his ankle improved a little every day. But his willpower? That was now limping along.

What came next? Topless pool therapy day?

Having a private pool suddenly seemed like a really legit reason for investing in real estate.

If he were into one-night stands, he'd find some woman to get naked with just to relieve the stress that spending every day with Grace in progressively smaller bathing suits was putting on his libido control.

"Not going to deny it?"

"Deny that I'm up to something?" The smile she gave him flashed so wickedly that he had to look anywhere but at her.

She maneuvered until she was beside him, facing in the same direction, and murmured, "You need to go a little deeper."

Deeper. Yes. Really…deep.

"Quit that," he bit out. "Just tell me what to do."

"Quit what?"

Like she didn't know what she was doing. "Don't play innocent with me. I'm onto you. Don't do that… provocative…well, it wasn't exactly dirty talk but you know we do that. Sexy double talk."

She pointed across his chest to the deeper end of the pool. "So you knew what I meant. Good. Move a little that way. The water should come up to your ribs. We're going to do some walking in the water. Back and forth here for a warm-up and then each time we'll move a little farther up the pool to progressively shallower water, so you'll be taking more weight on it each time. See how far you can go up. Then the same thing tomorrow."

"Is this the new measurement system?"

"Yes. Your range of motion is greatly improved so now we're working on slowly increasing strength."

"And are you going to admit what you're up to?" He asked the question but started walking in that slow, mostly submerged, bouncy fashion across the short length of the pool, staying in the same water depth.

She stayed beside him as he did as instructed, like he needed help or a safety net. Would it be better or worse if she were out of the pool and he got a view of her skimpy bikini every time he came toward her?

"You want a confession?"

"Yes." He stopped at the other side of the pool and turned around to start the return trip.

"I thought you didn't want to know all the details of what's going on in my head."

Frustration reaching snapping point, Liam paused long enough to brace his good leg against the bottom of the pool for support.

Grace stopped and looked at him, concern in her eyes.

Before she could say anything, he grabbed her by the waist, jumped as high as he could, and chucked her a few feet away from him in the water. He'd thrown that woman in the pool more times than he could count as teenagers. Usually in more shallow water, or from the side of the pool, where he could really get a good fling on her and send her flying. The ribs-deep water made that harder, but she still went under with a satisfying splash.

When she came up sputtering and laughing, he nodded and continued walking. "I don't. But apparently it's the only way through this. So out with it."

"I'm done playing it safe," Grace said, still smiling from the reminder of their old, more innocent games, as she approached him again to resume walking.

"That means what?"

"That means that I've realized that just because I'm afraid of losing again it doesn't mean that I can live with myself if I don't try."

"You should be able to." God help him, he wasn't going to make this easy on her. She had to get the idea to stop. "It isn't going to work. No matter how nice it might be. It can't."

Grace took a deep breath and as they reached the edge of the pool, ushered him about a foot higher, into somewhat more shallow water. "Again," she said, dealing with the therapy first while working out what she wanted to say. Considering the way they'd been circling one another for days, she hadn't expected him to approach this head-on. He wanted it all out in the open again, or so he claimed. No matter how badly that had gone last time. And she was completely out of instincts on it. It had all boiled down to simple facts: he enjoyed kissing her. He'd wanted her then, he still did now. That wasn't going to change because she found her spine again and tried to convince him.

"I've spent years wanting that night to have gone differently and I want to know. I want my night. With you."

"Grace—"

"Just wait. I know what you're going to say. We can't because of Nick, who I'm sure is putting just as much— if not more—pressure on you than he has been on me to stay apart. He said you're a player and I will just get hurt. Just like your last girlfriend was."

"He's right. About us. You're built for forever, and I won't ever marry. It's not for me. So you would get hurt."

"You're not a player. You're a serial dater, but you're not a player. You have relationships, otherwise they couldn't end up badly and in the news. The only reason I was news was because of how recently you broke up with Simone Andre, and because now she's in rehab."

One thing to be thankful for. At least Grace didn't

sound like she blamed him for Simone's drug problem, but he didn't want her thinking that. It didn't have anything to do with them, but he didn't want her to see him as recent gossip had been painting him.

"The stuff about Simone isn't true. I didn't just get done with her and move on. I didn't break her heart and turn her into an addict. I broke up with her because she *was* an addict. And I wanted her to get help. And she has. She's in rehab and I'm really glad, but, like I told you before, rumors and gossip spring up about everything, even stuff that isn't true. I don't need to make her life worse, and she's not the one telling people all this, so I don't correct the idiotic stories I see that paint me as the bad guy. Right now, I'm the stronger one. I can carry this for her. I can handle lies, it's the true stuff that hurts."

"You're making assumptions about what is best for me. You and Nick both are, and I'm a big girl. I can make my own decisions. I made some admittedly stupid choices in the past, but I was a bit younger then, you know. And we've already talked about being young and stupid. So that argument doesn't hold water, and you're doing me a disservice when you act like I need to be protected from you or that it's your job or Nick's job to do it."

"Got it. You don't need to be protected from me. But, to be clear, I would try and protect Nick from making a bad decision too if I knew in advance he was trying to make one. So I can't get mad at him for doing the same thing with me."

"Because you're about to make a bad decision with me?"

"That's what it looks like to Nick. I did make a bad decision in the limo."

"My point is, I would regret it more if I didn't try

to finish this than if we go to bed once and you never speak to me again. I'm pretty sure that you're never going to speak to me again anyway when this is all said and done. So what would you regret more?"

He stopped once more at the edge and gestured toward the shallow end again.

She nodded. "One more and then maybe we'll stay there for a couple of passes. This one worked your ankle a bit."

"This isn't too bad."

"It sounds like you're in pain, though." In pain and angry. Maybe she should just let this alone. She'd made her point. She'd put herself out there, and at least she'd done it with who she was this time.

"A little." At least he admitted to the physical feelings, and moved another foot down and shaved another few inches off the water depth. "And all that stuff I told you about my limits because of your family and our history?"

"I'm not going to announce it to Nick or Mom and Dad, Liam." She kept pace with him, letting him set the speed now. "I'm not going to go whining when it ends. I know I don't fit into your world. It's going to be over between us when you're recovered, one way or another. You're going off to some film location and, sure, you might send greetings through Nick in the future or ask how I'm doing, but we're not friends." She touched his arm, stopping him in the middle, forcing him to look at her.

"We're not friends anymore, Liam. Right now, we're pretending to be friends because if this attraction wasn't between us, we would be friends. I genuinely like you, and I know you like me. I know you care about me, and you care about my family, and our history... But it's never going to be what it was when we were kids. If it ever was that anyway. I can't be friends with you without all this between us."

Liam watched her in a way that said her words had been in his mind before she'd said them, and she watched as he reached up to rub the back of his neck. The man shouldn't have told her that body language tell. He felt emotionally in danger, that's what he'd said men did when they felt that.

"So it's going to end because of all the reasons we've talked about. Why is that going to be easier than if we've made one amazing memory together first?" She stepped back, one step, then another, her courage abandoning her at the end of her forward, angry confession. Now she had no choice but to flee if she wanted to keep breathing or keep from protecting her jugular notch.

Every time he said he wanted her honesty, it went like this, with his words drying up and her left trying to fill the gap.

"I want you to do another three passes here, back and forth. And then swim. Gently, not like you're being chased by sharks. Kick and flex your feet separately or together like a fish, but don't frog-kick your legs. Use your feet better, and don't overdo it. Do the same thing three times tomorrow. Morning, afternoon, and evening."

"Are you leaving?" he said finally, stopping in the center of the pool where she'd left him, the water lapping at his hips.

"Yes." If there was any fairness in the universe, he wouldn't hear her voice wobbling. "I'll see you in two days at the clinic. Text me what time you want to come. Morning, I'm guessing. Which would be fine. Or night. I can come back or stay late from work. If you want to meet at night, then do the exercises that day before you come, and we'll switch things when you get there."

He nodded, apparently not disagreeing with any of it.

She turned and headed for the side of the pool where her towel was, and kicked out of it.

The bikini business had to stop.

If anything were going to happen between them now, it had to be his move. Her cards were on the table. So many cards. God, what was she thinking?

Shaking the towel out, she wrapped it under her arms and clutched it there to head for the changing area.

Dry off. Get out. Go home.

Find some way to stop her words from playing on repeat all night. No rewind fantasies this time.

She couldn't take it if he once more failed to live up to them.

CHAPTER NINE

TIME TICKED ON. Grace met with Liam daily to check on him, changed his exercise regimen and measured his progress every other day. The days that she didn't see him he still came in to use the pool. Exercise in only his hotel's pool limited his ability to exercise several times a day so lately he'd spent more time there than the twenty minutes she prescribed three times a day.

And not once in all that time had Liam's poker face slipped an inch. She had no idea whether or not her words to him had made a difference, all she knew was that she was out of gumption to chase things.

Three days ago she'd added dry-ground exercises to his program, in addition to the pool strengthening techniques. They'd see him through to the start of his first project, and he'd reached the point that he didn't need monitoring. That meant today he was being discharged from supervised rehabilitation.

Grace stepped out of her office, clipboard in hand with the discharge paperwork snapped in, and headed to the pool therapy room, hoping to catch him before he got into the water.

"Liam?" She called him out of the locker room.

Hearing a splash, she turned back to the pool in time to see him rising above the closest edge, every muscle in the man's arms and chest flexed, the tattoos he bore on his shoulder rippling in some breath-catching combination of strength and water running off tanned skin.

The clipboard in her hand felt as heavy as her tongue.

This was it. This moment was the end of whatever insanity they'd been cycling through for the past three weeks. She'd talked to him before about the papers, now she just had to find some way to remind him. Some words to say.

She had nothing.

He was going to let it go without a backward glance. She was probably already in his rearview mirror.

Spinning the clipboard paper side out, she gave it a little shake and then laid it on a nearby bench with the pen.

There. Message delivered.

She showed him her keys too as farewell, then turned and hurried out.

Someone else would lock up. They stayed late. She needed to go.

At least this time it wasn't humiliation eating a hole in her, even if he clearly didn't want her as badly as she wanted him.

Whatever it was could just remain undefined. She didn't have any energy left to roll it around in her mind. Not when there was wine chilling in her fridge and yoga pants waiting for her.

A knock on the door interrupted Grace's night of sulking and drinking.

She flopped back against the plush pillows on her couch and stared at the ceiling.

It was probably Nick. Yesterday, when she'd called him to catch up, she'd refused to talk about Liam and had hoped that would be the end of it, but that's never how things went with her protective older brother.

At least since her accident. Before that mess he'd pretty much left her to her own devices when it came to the guys she dated. Which probably informed his protectiveness now because no matter if she chose hot bad boys to date, they were never good for her. And they were never a good enough stand-in for Liam for her to keep playing that game when it became clear to her how fragile her hold on this life could be.

Another knock came, but no yelling. Not Nick.

She took another drink of her wine to fortify herself, and to empty her third glass, set it down and peel herself up off the couch.

Emboldened by booze, she flipped off one security device after another, locks and stoppers designed to allow her to peek without subjecting herself to the danger of a full door opening.

But the security in her building was too good for that to be a real issue.

She flung the door open and there Liam stood.

Or leaned, one shoulder resting against her doorjamb, hair wet and disheveled, his black T-shirt clinging to him like he'd not taken the time to even dry himself properly before throwing his clothes on and coming to find her.

The heat and hunger in his eyes sent sparks licking all over her body and burned away any doubts she'd been nursing through her second glass of wine.

Once again she was struck by her inability to predict this man.

"I don't have a trench coat," he said finally when she'd failed to come up with even a single word of greeting. "Can I come in anyway?"

Instead of answering, Grace reached directly for his belt and dipped her fingers into the front of his jeans. Soft hair brushed the backs of her fingers and she closed her hand around the buckle to tug him insistently through her apartment door.

One step inside and she launched herself against him, arms flying around his shoulders as she pressed as close as she could get, hungry mouth glued to his.

He managed to close the door and flip some locks, then she was against the wall, the tank top she'd donned to laze around the house inched up. Soon her belly burned with the heat of his firm, muscled torso against her.

More. She wanted more skin, the only thought strong enough to barrel through years of need coiling in her belly.

When her shirt reached her arms she let go of Liam long enough for him to whisk the material over her head.

He tossed the flimsy tank top and then stepped away from her, his eyes rolling down her body, which heated her skin too, just not as well as his skin against hers.

She once more closed the distance between them, needing his flesh against her. Before she could slide her arms around his shoulders once more, his hands landed on her hips and he pressed her back against the wall, falling to one knee as he did so.

He was going to hurt himself. A trickle of rationality made it through her fuzzy brain. "Your ankle." The get-up he had on might be meant to tantalize, but he'd still known better than to take off the boot cast he'd been in since they'd returned from New York.

"It's fine," he said, pressing his face against the flat plane of her belly, then trailing wet kisses from one hip to the other, the stubble he wore so well rasping along her skin.

When he dug his fingers into the waist of the pants and dragged them down, along with the flimsy panties, she realized his intention.

No sooner had they wrestled her legs from the cotton tangle than he had one of her legs over his shoulder and his hot mouth pressed into her.

His tongue stroked and his lips plucked as if he were starved for her, as if he'd spent every night for the past six years dreaming of exactly this. She couldn't tell whose moans were louder.

All she could do was grab the frame of her front door for support as pleasure blazed through her, arching her back so hard she would've fallen without his hands clamped to her hips.

The fervor with which he loved told her he wasn't stopping until he'd wrung her out for their first course.

All the bad boys she'd dated…there could be no comparison. It might not be her first time but deep inside, for that girl who'd yearned for him for so long, it was her first time.

But she needed to touch him so, sparing one hand, she plowed her fingers through his hair, down that tattooed shoulder and the muscled arm…until she found the hand that held her hip. Instinctively, her fingers wrapped around the first digit she could get hold of.

Connection completed, the orgasm given by his greedy mouth almost split her in two.

The name that had secretly echoed in her heart for every lover finally passed her lips. She cried his name, and then again. And again.

When the last spasm burst, her supporting leg buckled, unwilling to hold her anymore.

Quickly, he turned the fall into a controlled slide, and once she touched the floor he crawled up her body, still hungry.

"Here?" He panted the question more than asked, eyeing the open window not ten feet away before he looked back down at her. "Not here."

"We're going to do this right. If it's the only time… and it is, right? You…you agree that it's the only time?" He pulled her up against him but stayed where he blocked the window.

When she nodded, he pulled his T-shirt off, baring that sculpted perfection that was his chest and belly. He wrapped the black cotton around her hips and tied the corners. "Then we need a bed. I want…everything to be perfect. Cool cotton sheets and pillows…"

"Bed. That way." Her words still slurred just a little, drunk with pleasure.

But she scrambled to her feet and offered him both her hands to tug him back up, her faculties slowly returning. "Use the booted foot to stand. The other one can bend…"

"Don't worry about my ankle," he said, but he still took her hand and did as she instructed. "It's fine."

She backed toward her room. Looking at him was too good. He didn't try to hide his want at all, and the front of his jeans strained over a heady ridge of flesh.

Oh, God, this was real. He was really there. Not just here in her mind, not a fantasy.

She didn't even want to know what had changed his mind. Later. She could ask later, or not. Maybe it would be better if they didn't talk about anything else, didn't get more attached. Just one time, and then…let it stay perfect in memories.

Don't think about after.

"My turn," she said, as they passed through the door into her room and she felt the edge of the bed against the backs of her legs and released his hands to let hers roam up and down over his chest, alternating gentle touches with little scratches anywhere she found hair. Down, over his belly, and she fell to her knees beside the bed.

"No. I can't wait. Next time." The words strangled in his throat, and it only took one look into his eyes for her to know the reason for it.

There would be no next time.

This was supposed to be a farewell.

The thought almost put her off the whole thing.

Almost.

Grace was a big girl. She was the master, not her emotions. And this had been her idea. Her only chance.

She unfastened his belt, unbuttoned his jeans and eased the zipper down, her eyes still locked on his.

"Please? Just for a moment?"

He read people, he knew what was on her mind. He could call the whole thing off; now would be the time…

The moment lengthened, with him clearly struggling with all this as much as she was. When he didn't say anything, she took his silence as consent and brought the head to her mouth, letting her lower lip rest against the crown, letting him stop her.

No stopping. He nodded, jerkily, and reached down to touch her face as the impressive manhood she held in her hands bobbed against her mouth.

"One night," he managed, as the heat of her mouth enfolded him. "I want the whole night."

She nodded, and she worked him deeper into her mouth, letting her tongue luxuriate in the slick skin and the salty evidence of his need. He slid his fingers into her hair, his eyes on hers, letting her see what every flick of her tongue did to him.

Right now he was hers, without barriers, and that was enough. It'd have to be enough.

It wasn't long before he gasped and gestured urgently, trying to pull himself free of her mouth. But she didn't want that, she wanted everything she could get from him tonight—her one and only night—and grabbed his hip and drank him down.

When she finally moved back, he collapsed onto the bed, hands closing on her arms to pull her up to him so that her cheek rested on his chest and he tangled one hand in her hair.

"No holding back. One night, no holding back," she whispered against his skin, kissing her way back down to his boot.

"Okay."

A couple of strategic Velcro rips and she had his foot free. "Thank God, you've got the bandage too. I don't think I could control my fingers enough to wrap it."

He laughed. "I'm already on the bed and I'm not sure if I can get up to the head of it."

She crawled up onto the bed, fetched condoms from the nightstand to have them within easy reach. "For when you're able."

He nodded, and just pulled her back to him, still struggling to catch his breath.

"Aren't you able yet? It's been at least fifteen seconds. I thought you had stamina." She couldn't stop herself from teasing. She wanted that too—no holding back meant giving everything, pleasure and passion and the playful side of both. That's who they were. That's what she wanted, the real Liam, not the polished celebrity adored by the masses.

He dragged himself more fully on the bed and reached for her. Soon they lay face-to-face, him on his good side—and she let him as it'd minimize the pressure on his ankle. "Can't have you doubting my stamina. But in my defense that was a cripplingly good orgasm. I might need a minute to get my mojo back."

His humor had returned to match her own. She couldn't stop herself smiling. "So long as you're not done."

"I'm far from done," he assured her, running his hand over her hip as if he couldn't quite believe that he had his hands on her. "I'm going to need at least two more rounds before I'm done. Maybe three. If you don't fall asleep."

"Me?" She laughed and scooted closer so that their noses all but touched. "Let me remind you that I'm the one who worked for this. Seducing you is exhausting, Mr. Carter."

He took her tease in the spirit it was offered, and slid his arms around her as she hooked a leg over his hip to keep him close, little adjustments to get closer and closer. She could already feel him growing hard again against her inner thigh.

His expression sobered a little. "I'm sorry. But you know it's not because I didn't want you. You wouldn't believe how I've imagined this. So long. You got me through some dark days, Gracie. Actually, this is probably going to sound pretty creepy, but when I was penniless in LA, doing all those awful jobs that got me from audition to audition, my favorite pastime was thinking of you. Off at school. Standing in front of that apartment door with the trench coat open and sheer black bra and panties...I could still draw a picture with every detail preserved. If I could draw."

"You pictured me a lot?"

"Every day."

"Just dark times?"

"No, of course not. Good times too. When I had some time alone. Going to sleep. Running."

"Was I the carrot?" she asked, leaning down to kiss him again, her fingers combing through his hair in a way that was both soothing and arousing at the same time. Increased pressure encouraged him to roll over, and she went with him.

"Sometimes," he murmured.

"Sometimes it was some other woman in her underwear?"

"No," he said, pushing her hair back from his face, the tenderness in his eyes making her inexplicably teary. "I don't think I've ever daydreamed about another woman like I do about you. But I don't always run happy. Sometimes…"

"Sometimes you run mad? Sad?"

"Yes. Though that doesn't always work out well. Running if you're too distracted can result in a sprained ankle."

Sprained ankle? She probably shouldn't ask, but it was right after he and his girlfriend had split. "Because of Simone?"

"No. No, not Simone." He slid a hand around the knee she had hooked over his hip and rolled to his back so that she was on top of him.

She sat up then, settling herself against him at the wrong end for penetration, but still in a place where she knew he'd enjoy a little friction.

"What were you upset about? The part?"

"No. Less talk. More… Where's the condom?"

"Not until you tell me what made you fall," she said,

flattening her hands against his chest and grinding her hips down just enough to slicken him.

His eyes got that unfocused look of pleasure and he grabbed her hips to keep her right there, even as he groaned his complaint. "Not fair."

"I don't play fair." She usually played fair, actually, but if it wasn't important, he wouldn't be trying to hide it. "No holding back. You agreed."

He sighed then and stopped her hips. "It was the anniversary of my father's death. It's always a bad day."

A bad day, he'd said. Like those words were powerful enough to carry all the meaning that went with them.

When she'd first met Liam she remembered thinking he was different, and the discussion she'd had with her parents about foster care, and why Liam was in foster care. Her parents had told her enough that she'd have been nice to him even if he hadn't been the most handsome boy she'd ever seen. But Liam wasn't much for sharing. He minimized things. And she was beginning to understand that the things he minimized most were the things that hurt the most.

"Did I kill the mood?"

Grace realized she'd been staring at him a long time and that she had tears in her eyes.

That no-holding-back rule... "Does that happen on your mother's anniversary too? Or were you too little when she died to really—?"

"I don't remember much about that." He lifted that tattooed shoulder, minimizing further.

"But you do remember your father's death. Were you there?"

"No. I found him later." His words were delivered so flatly and emotionlessly...

Her heart ached, her eyes burned, and she leaned forward to kiss him, unable to say anything.

Warmth slid up her body as his hands crept to her cheeks, and as he accepted and returned every wet kiss, his thumbs brushed away her tears.

When she'd kissed him enough to give him a glimpse of all the sorrow she felt on his behalf, she leaned up to look at him again. The tears still came, but his eyes were dry.

"Don't cry. I'm okay now. You got me better."

"It's not that. It's not that you got distracted and fell. Can't I just be heartbroken for you? Because I am."

"I'm not."

Lies. Lies he might have even believed.

He reached to the side, grabbing one of the foil packets she'd put out and tearing it open as he sat up, pushing her up as he did so, freeing the erection once captured between them for the condom.

"Liam…"

"Do you still have those panties and that bra?"

"No."

She knew what he was doing. He'd done what he'd promised, he hadn't held back, but now he was getting this fantasy-fulfilling evening back on course.

"I went home and burned them. They were all tainted with unrequited longing and…"

A little shifting and she felt herself stretching to accommodate the hardness pushing insistently into her.

"Do you have some other ones? I think… I deserve some black underwear to complete this memory."

She wanted another night. Another ten thousand nights wouldn't be enough.

CHAPTER TEN

ANYTHING SHE WANTED. After their night, when they'd both been drunk on pleasure and each other, when the idea that everything would be okay somehow had dominated his mind, Liam had announced he'd give her whatever she wanted. Ask him anything, he'd say yes.

And he had. Even when she'd asked him to be her date to a wedding.

So dumb. All of that was going to make this harder. Consequences.

Liam tossed his keys to the valet and went to offer Grace his elbow. The boot that made it easy to walk without support didn't go with his formal wear, so he was back to tape and a cane. Only today it didn't hurt much at all with the tape. Unlike before. A sign of progress: that he'd healed enough for tape to work. At least physically, though his heart and conscience were starting to feel battered from the effort.

He looked down at her smiling face and the pit of acid eating a hole through him widened, and he had to work to swallow it down. Whatever was between them was usually flirty and playful. Even when she'd been grumpy with him over his ankle, they'd still found their way back to that playful relationship.

And there was the problem word. They no longer had one fantastic night, they had a relationship.

This was a date.

A date to a wedding, of all things. Because Grace was made for the fairy tale.

He should have figured out some way out of that promise. But he'd considered it, and the fact that they'd be staying alone together in a hotel had overridden his sensibilities. One night had turned into one more night.

But he hated broken promises, with all the promises made and broken in his childhood, so making promises lightly should be the last thing he'd ever do.

And the Liam from Grace's bed—the one satisfied down to every last atom—would've kept that promise. So today, even though he'd had two days to come to the conclusion that this was a bad idea, he had to keep his promise to Grace. He just couldn't keep it well. The spirit of the promise was different from the tangible semantics of it.

Tonight had to end differently than she wanted. It had to end differently than even he wanted. Because what he wanted was the opposite from what was right. Tonight had to be a bad night. To help her see things clearly. To knock the stars from her eyes.

She gasped softly as they walked through the lit estate. Cool night breezes rolled off the ocean below and all the trees glittered with white lights.

"I guess this is what the wedding of the children of Hollywood royalty looks like," Grace murmured, squeezing his arm. "Your ankle okay?"

"It's fine."

"Are you sure? You look like you're in pain."

"I'm okay."

"You're scowling," she said, waving with her free hand to different people they passed.

Security took their names, and an usher came to escort them off to more white and gold, to rows of chairs in two blocks facing an astonishingly lit gazebo and a sea of puffy white flower balls that Liam couldn't identify.

"I'm..." He started to deny it, but then lowered his voice and his head to her so no one else would hear. "I'm not a fan of weddings."

"But it looks like a fairy tale."

Fairy tale.

Seated, Liam shifted around, trying to get comfortable. "Yes. It does."

"You're not happy for Freya and Zack?"

"Don't know Zack, but sure. Freya's a good person." Liam didn't know her well, but they'd spoken a few times at some event or another. It was impossible to move in the same circles for years and not interact on some level. He had gone to The Hollywood Hills Clinic because it was attached to the Rothsbergs, after all. "She's smart and she's worked for what she has. So, sure. This is what they want? I'm happy for them."

Grace leaned back a touch, studying him. Since they'd been around one another for this second chance...or whatever it was...she'd watched him study people. Been told a few too many times what she was thinking because he studied her. And she'd picked up a thing or two.

He'd carefully positioned himself on the chair beside her so that they weren't touching. His arms were crossed as he waited and other guests were shown to seats around them, and he didn't even look at her when he spoke.

Liam didn't just not want to be there, he didn't want to be there with her.

Or was it a case of him not wanting to be there with her in front of people who moved in his circles? She only moved in adjacent circles that had some people who moved in his circles...

Her blue dress was nice but not designer. It fit her well, but wasn't couture. She hadn't gone to a stylist to have her hair and makeup done. She hadn't paid a week's salary for her shoes or her handbag. And the simple diamond teardrop necklace she wore for special occasions wasn't big enough to be specially insured. She looked nice, but far from glamorous.

Liam, on the other hand, wore a handmade suit. His shoes were probably also made just for his feet. And he smelled like sin, but who even knew if that was a cologne or just the way he smelled? Not her.

So was it the family thing again? Somehow, after their night together, she'd thought he was coming around to that. Nick wouldn't be at the wedding. There were so many people there that even if camera crews gatecrashed, it wouldn't be to see if Liam had brought his physical therapist again. No one in her family had to know yet, so it couldn't be the circumstances tonight. It was about Liam not feeling it between them, even though she knew this path had to be leading somewhere if he'd just walk it with her.

Off to one side of the gazebo, musicians lifted their instruments and began to play. As the groom and groomsmen stepped up into the twinkling gazebo, beautiful string music began to fill the air.

She reached up and touched Liam's elbow, causing him to turn and look at her finally. "It's starting. You might not want to keep your arms crossed. It sends the wrong impression."

Everyone rose, so they did as well. Liam's arms unfolded to hang at his sides, but tension still screamed from his frame. She should have stood at the end, at least then she wouldn't be looking over his broad-shouldered surliness to see Freya in her dress.

Well, his surliness wasn't going to ruin the wedding for her. She wouldn't let it.

Unlike Liam, Grace loved weddings. She loved them even more when they seemed built to last rather than just being another notch in the bedpost of some star.

As Freya passed their row, it was impossible to miss her glow. She belonged there under the twinkling lights. Radiant in her pregnancy, the twins she carried only added to her blessings.

When they sat again, Liam kept his eyes forward, but at least he didn't cross his arms again.

She had to stop looking at him.

No matter what she felt, no matter what she believed could be theirs, it didn't matter if he didn't see it too.

She really had to stop trying to be with him. Leaving a door open to him was just as bad, she'd be the only one aware of it and waiting for him to come back through if she did.

They'd said one night, but it had been such a wonderful night, when he'd said yes to anything, she'd wanted to believe he felt it too.

He'd probably just felt the need to shut her up so he could sleep.

Six years hadn't made her any smarter about relationships.

The ceremony was crafted of beautiful words, and

all around her Grace saw handkerchiefs out and plenty
of eye dabbing.

Did Zack take Freya? Yes. He did.

Did Freya take Zack? Yes.

They kissed.

Loving, honoring, cherishing. Forever. Not just one
night. Not just one night that got dragged into two by
one pushy person. But the beauty she could identify
she didn't feel. By the time it was over, all she could
do was force a smile.

That's what her situation with Liam lacked: they
weren't both in it. She was the only one there, waiting
for him to make up his mind.

The wedding party walked back down the aisle, and
Grace stood, clapped with the rest of them.

Eventually they moved from the site of the wedding
up the stairs built into the hillside to another plateau,
this time at the top. The large cliff-top oceanside over-
look had been set up to host the reception. Dinner. Marble checkerboard slabs defining a dance floor. Candles
twinkling on every table, and an open wood frame-
work above supported thousands more of the twinkling
white lights. More stars in the sky than ever for Zack
and Freya.

Perfection.

"Bar," Liam said, drawing her attention back to him
with one word and gesturing hand. He pulled his elbow
from her limp grasp and started away, saying as he left,
"Find our seats?"

Find our seats? That implied he'd come and find her
when he'd dulled his senses with bourbon or something
higher proof if he could find that instead.

This evening couldn't end fast enough.

Grace turned to survey the tables to decide where

to start looking. She wasn't really one of the elite, she just worked with them. She wouldn't be seated at the kiddie table, but it would no doubt be farther from the action than Liam would've been had his name been the one on the list and she'd been his plus one.

Like that would've ever happened.

The cheerful sound of people laughing and chattering hurt her head, and the whole situation hurt her heart.

She checked a few of the peripheral tables, found her name, and pulled out the chair.

Time to fake a smile and sit with him through the dinner. Time to pretend for the benefit of everyone else, so she didn't come off as one of those women who became depressed at weddings. If he hadn't driven them there, maybe she could just go and give her love and her congratulations to the couple and tell Liam they could go. Another reason why it would've been better to have stayed dateless for the occasion.

Was he still taking the pain medication?

Was it her place to ask if he was mixing alcohol and his anti-inflammatories?

No. He wasn't her patient anymore. And he clearly didn't want to be more.

This was what came from her making bold moves in Relationshipville. She should have just been happy to have gotten him into bed. She'd had her night. And it had been so good it had made her stupid. Her IQ always seemed to drop a few points where Liam Carter was concerned.

She forced a smile as people joined her, introduced herself, made the expected small talk. Eventually, Liam came over, placed a drink on the table for her and took his seat beside her, much to the delight of everyone at the table except Grace.

Drinking the fruity concoction gave her a cover for not being chatty and personable. Liam was the one everyone wanted to talk to anyway, and it suited her.

She'd muddled through difficult situations before. She'd survived being rejected in her underwear, she could handle this rejection too. But it would've been nice if it had come before the wedding. Then she could pretend easier.

By the time the dancing rolled around she was so ready to go but had to wait until the bride and groom were off the dance floor.

"Pardon me," she murmured to the table at large, scooted her chair back and wound her way through the tables to the clearing and into a copse of trees on the far side.

Just a moment alone. That's all she needed. Somewhere quieter to breathe.

She wandered through the trees until she got to the edge of the cliff, out of sight, somewhere she could see the water, and leaned over.

Now what?

It wasn't long until she made out the sound of movement in the trees behind her. And voices. At first quiet, but then loud enough for her to recognize one.

James Rothsberg.

And he was talking to a woman.

Grace leaned around the tree just enough to see who was there, and considered her escape route.

This was what came from her going to the edge, there was nowhere to go besides over the cliff into the water and rocks far below, or past James and...

"Mila, you look good."

Moonlight filtered through the treetops, a shaft illuminating the woman's face. Romantic.

Oh, hell.

Grace leaned back again, looking at the ledge between the trees and the cliff face.

Was that wide enough for her to skirt the trees without plummeting to her death in her high heels?

The last thing she wanted was to see her boss having A Moment. Especially tonight. Could she not get away from the magic in the air anywhere?

"Do I? I looked better at our wedding."

Their wedding? Okay, maybe it wasn't going to be that kind of a moment.

Grace couldn't stop herself. She had to look again.

Should she clear her throat? Climb the trees and see if she could get in touch with her inner primate and balance-beam her way across the limbs without breaking her neck?

There was some talk of another woman, which Grace didn't entirely catch.

But then Mila raised her voice. "I don't care who you're dating. Or who you're not dating. Or who you're maybe thinking of one day dating. It's not my business anymore. My business is Bright Hope and my patients, that's what's most important to me now. Let's leave it at that."

"A truce, then?"

"I haven't been picking fights with you, James."

"I'm not picking a fight either, but that's how things keep going. So…truce. Let's just try to keep things professional."

"Yes. That's what I've been trying to get across to you."

"And once the photo shoot for the South LA Clinic is done, we'll just keep to our separate corners. No need for further interaction."

"Sounds good."

Grace could feel the emotion tingling in the woman's voice, but considering this wedding business and another woman…well, who could blame her for being roused to a quiet fight with her ex?

James and Mila had once been married, or something…and now they were stuck working together? Maybe not smoothly working together but they were trying. She knew she'd heard the word "truce" in there. Because that was the adult way to handle these kinds of relationship issues.

Which made her hiding in the trees until it was time to leave clearly not the adult way to handle this mess with Liam.

Freya wouldn't notice if she slipped out before face-to-face congratulations, she had so much else going on this evening.

Grace peeked around her hiding tree again, but no longer saw James or Mila so she darted through the trees and back to the reception.

Get Liam.

Get out of there.

And just get it over with.

She should've stuck with just the one night.

Liam hadn't expected her to want to leave before the first dance but, then, she probably wouldn't have let him dance on his ankle. And she'd spent so much time away after dinner it seemed like his plan to make her dump him was working.

His stomach soured at the thought.

But if she did the leaving this time, she wouldn't feel rejected. It would be her turn. And he could take it.

With her silent and tense at his side, Liam opened the door to their hotel room and held it for her.

Grace stepped past him and went straight to the mini-bar. Ten seconds later she'd poured herself a straight vodka and in less time than it took for her to lift the glass to her mouth the clear liquid was gone.

The drink must've burned as she breathed hard, coughed a little, and put the glass down. Pulling her shoulders back first, she turned around to face him.

"I don't know how to do this. Never thought it would come to this, but it's just one more way I'm delusional when it comes to you." She stopped, rubbed her head and paced away from him, then back.

Self-comforting. Dispelling tension.

It was happening. He could smell it in the air like salt by the ocean. His stomach rolled and he stuffed his hands into his pockets, lest she see him shaking.

Unlike the dinner where he'd brought up the trench coat, she wasn't hiding her gaze from him tonight. It was all right there, spelled out for him.

"Whatever stupid idea made me invite you tonight, consider me over it. I thought that things changed between us that night. I thought that you had finally stopped running from this. I thought you felt..." The words dried in her throat, and she looked back at the empty glass. "Something."

"It was supposed to be one night," he said, avoiding all that talk of feelings, because even now, even though this was what had to happen, he wanted to comfort her.

"I know!" Grace blurted out. "I know that's what we'd said. But that was before we were together, and one time became one night, became one whole night, became yes to whatever I wanted. That was the perfect example of a situation changing, right? It seemed that way. It seemed like..."

She stopped facing him and went to the balcony doors and opened them, pulling the drapes back so that the cool night air could blow in, and breathed deeply.

He didn't know what to say, aside from the apology clawing at the back of his throat. He shut his mouth so she'd keep going, make it go just as he'd rehearsed in his mind all day.

"I didn't ask you to come with me because I was trying to collar you. I haven't been writing 'Mrs. Grace Carter' on my notebooks. I just wanted to be with you and see how things went. I didn't invite you here as some grand gesture to hint for you to start making commitments. I know that there are extenuating circumstances to be careful of with my family. And I know you're just out of a relationship."

"That relationship has nothing to do with this one."

"No? Because you don't care what people say about you and Simone?"

"No. I care about what your family could say about us. That would be true. Unless this leads to marriage, then it's a betrayal of the trust that David and Lucy put in me when they welcomed me into your home."

"Why?"

Damn. She was going off script. This wasn't how it was supposed to go. She was supposed to yell and leave. Demanding explanations meant she saw through his tactics, and there was a danger of this turning into him rejecting her again.

"Because you're built for marriage, Grace. You are a cry-through-the-ceremony woman. But I don't want to be married. Not ever. I don't want kids. Any of it. I am not your white-picket-fence future. But that's what you want, or what you'd come to want, because that's who you are. And you would get hurt."

"I'm hurt now! Because you're lying to yourself and to me. I love you, and I know you love me."

Rolling stomach turned to nausea at her words. Ignore it. Ignore them. He drew a deep breath, looked her in the eye, and said, "I don't love you. Not like that."

The words felt like mud in his mouth. Mud and blood. Acidic and wrong.

She shook her head, tears in her eyes. "Yes, you do. You might not want marriage and children, but you feel more for me than lust. I'm not nothing to you."

"I never said you were nothing to me. But even if I did love you, love doesn't make things magically work out. My parents loved one another. They did. They probably loved me too in some twisted way—why else would my father refuse to grant permission for me to be adopted for so long but to keep from losing me? They were full of love, for each other, for me, and for their heroin. They still spiraled into death and destruction together."

How had this gone so far off course? There was no easy way out of it. No one else had forced him to say words he'd never wanted to give voice to, there was no one else he felt compelled to bare his soul to. Another reason to get out now.

She poured herself another drink.

"I loved my father, Grace. I loved him and I still couldn't save him. When Nick went to school and I moved into my own place in LA? Before my acting took off, I sought him out, moved him in with me. I thought maybe if he was there and we had a relationship, if he had someone to count on, someone to talk with about Mom, I thought he could heal. But he didn't.

He died, Grace. He died alone on the living room floor of my run-down little hovel. Love didn't help him. Not once. Not ever. Love doesn't fix things, it just makes losing harder."

The tears in her eyes spilled over her cheeks and she stepped toward him, her instinct to comfort him. Always to comfort. Even when they were fighting.

"I'm sorry," she whispered, stopping before she got to him, lowering the hands that had half reached for his face. "Your love couldn't fix him. Are you telling me this now because you want me to come around to the notion that my love can't fix you?"

"Yes." He felt his heart hammering against his chest. "I'd ruin you. That's what I'm built for. That's the example I have to draw from."

"You're wrong."

"I'm not."

"Yes, you are, because you don't need fixing. You didn't kill your father or your mother. Fate handed you a terrible situation, and you survived it. And you learned to thrive. You didn't ruin Simone. You didn't use me and throw me away, even when we were stupid kids and I offered you everything. You tried to do what was honorable at that time, you tried it later. I know you're trying now, but it just so happens that you're wrong." Her voice stayed confident and certain until she got to the end, and then it broke. One aborted sob followed by a short, bitter laugh—a sound nothing like the full-throated laughter he loved to hear from her. "Don't feel bad about it. I keep screwing up with you too."

"You give me too much credit. I agreed to one night with you because I crave you like an addict craves heroin. And you have the same addiction. I didn't care. Even now, I don't care. I want to stay because I want to be with you, but for the need to do better by you than what I learned from them. And if we keep on the way we want to there would eventually be a child. Or you'd want one. And people learn from their parents' example. My parents were abusive, neglectful junkies. Is that what you want for your children?"

"That's not what would happen. I saw you with Brody. But if you want to blame someone for this situation, then blame me. I'm the one who couldn't let go. And if you're guilty of anything, it's being too afraid to take a risk on me. I'm not afraid to take a risk on you. I know a sure thing when I see it. You might not see it, and I don't think you even want to see it, but you're an honorable man, Liam. Or else you'd still be with Simone."

Grace swiped her cheeks, picked up her handbag and then went to grab the handle of her suitcase.

"Where are you going?" His palms started to sweat and the air felt thick, soupy, hard to breathe.

"We're broken up, right? I can't stay here with you in this hotel room." She unlocked and opened the door. "Take care of yourself, Liam. You couldn't save your father, what happened to him was due to his own decisions. And I can't save you from this, because it's your decision. Only you can save yourself. Don't just do it in your rewind fantasies of this evening, and don't take too long... I'm not going to wait for you forever, even though I know that's how long I'll love you."

She pulled the door open, her head up and her shoulders back. And she was gone.

CHAPTER ELEVEN

SWIMMING IN THE pool at work had rules, and one of those rules was the hours of operation. But at two thirty in the morning, after tossing and turning her sheets into a sweaty tangle, those rules meant very little even to the perennially law-abiding.

The last place Grace wanted to be was somewhere she'd spent so much time with Liam, but work was the only place she could find a pool where she knew it would be safe to swim alone at that hour.

It took a little explaining to get her past the guard, but as she flipped on the lights to the pool room she could already feel the stress starting to abate.

A swim was what she needed. Exercise to burn off excess energy. The comfort of the familiar. Maybe the water could give her even the metaphorical weightlessness she wanted, some way to return to her usual mental and emotional buoyancy.

She dove in and prayed the water would work its usual magic on her.

How long had it taken her to get over Liam the first time? Really get over him, not just take out her frustrations by kissing every cute boy who hadn't immediately bored her?

Well, that was a depressing thought.

Because she'd never got over Liam. Not really.

She had eventually got to a place where it had hurt less and she hadn't cringed when she'd heard his name. By the time his face had been plastered everywhere, it hadn't even really hurt anymore. She'd built up a callus, which she'd vigorously exfoliated when she'd gotten tangled up with him again.

Kicking harder, she turned under the water, completing her first lap.

Three days and she hadn't heard anything from Liam. Tonight she'd come to the conclusion that she wouldn't. The paparazzi who'd found out where she worked had mostly given up following her—all except for a couple intermittent stragglers. Why bother watching her when Liam was clearly nowhere around? She went to work. She went home. She swam. It wasn't terribly interesting.

Even if they saw what she did when she was home, it would probably only inspire pity in them.

She was considering getting some cats.

And learning a craft of some kind.

And moving in with people who shunned cell phones. Anything to keep herself from asking Nick about Liam. He'd stopped talking about his friend anymore when they spoke, and she didn't know if Nick and Liam were even speaking to each other.

If they weren't on speaking terms any longer, that would mean that her desires had interfered with her brother's relationships. And if they were, it would be just as awkward between her and Nick, even if it was a different kind of awkward.

Cats, crafts, and shunning technology seemed like the safest outlets to turn her attention to.

Or maybe it was time for a change of scenery. Take

another job with a sports team, somewhere other than California, New York, or Virginia. Maybe if she went far enough away, she could figure out how to put it all behind her.

Liam sat sideways on the sofa in his hotel suite, trying to wrap his ankle before his guest arrived. It had probably gotten to the point that he could stop wearing all the wraps and splints if he was careful, but he'd be cautious a little longer. He just couldn't call Grace up and ask her.

He couldn't call Grace up for any reason.

But Nick he had called, and Liam was now waiting for his oldest friend to arrive. With all that had gone on with Grace, and then with Nick's reaction, he needed to figure out where they stood.

By the time he worked the little metal thing into the bandage to keep it in place, the door opened and Nick strolled in. "Hey, Miles let me in. He said you were working on your ankle."

Nick stopped by the sofa and looked down at the bandaged limb. "That looks like the same technique you use to wrap gifts."

"I don't wrap gifts anymore. Hailey does it now," Liam said, dragging a smile on his face even if it was just for show right now. He used to also have someone who would wrap his ankle for him, but that was over. And the reason why seeing Nick for the first time in more than a month felt like walking to an execution he'd volunteered for. "Thanks for coming. Want a drink? Bar's stocked, as always."

Liam got his sword cane and used it to meander over to the bar. Talking at the bar felt better than talking on the sofa. Less intimate, and Nick wasn't the Watson who Liam had a history of getting intimate with.

Nick followed and reached for the Scotch and two short tumblers. A minute later they had ice and whiskey in them. Liam had given up the pain relievers last week, just in time for this conversation that required alcohol.

"So, do you want to talk about my sister?" Nick slid a glass to him.

Right to the point.

Liam nodded, took a drink of the Scotch and looked for the words. Unlike with the Trench Coat talk, he hadn't planned any of this beforehand. He was by turns apologetic with Nick and angry with him, but before he got to his apologies, there were things he needed to know.

"Yes. And I asked you here because you're my best friend so if there isn't honesty with us, then this friendship isn't worth saving."

"Is there some reason it's going to be in jeopardy?"

"You might think so after I tell you what happened with your sister." Liam downed the Scotch and slid the glass back to Nick with a nod to refill it. "But first I need to know something."

Nick didn't sit. He stayed standing on the other side of the bar where the booze could be easily reached. "I think I know what happened with my sister. You dated her. You kissed her. You said you weren't going to do anything else, and then you ended up at a wedding with her. So I'm guessing that something else happened in there somewhere."

"Something else happened."

Another two fingers of booze slid back to him and Liam took another good pull at it—they always stocked the good stuff at this hotel, but this bottle could be smashed over his head just as successfully as rotgut.

"More happened. A lot happened. But, speaking of things that happened... You've known about her feelings for me for a long time. So I have to ask—when she had her accident and was in the hospital, why did you never tell me? She's got scars, she said that a motorcycle wreck derailed her from her career goals, and I would swear on a stack of bibles that you never said one word to me about her getting hurt."

"That's because I didn't." Nick rubbed the back of his neck and then leaned on the bar. "Your dad died that day, Liam."

It was a week and two days since the wedding, Grace spent most of her evenings alone with wine and movies. Tonight she'd added her cell phone, and now sat replaying a voice mail over and over, with her thumb hovering over the delete button, unable to bring it down.

Liam's bosses—the producers and whoever she'd spoken to on the phone about him—had called to offer her a job on their set.

High action, medieval, dragon-chasing fantasies could injure the actors and stunt crew just as effectively as thrillers and movies where the good guys fought the bad guys with high-speed chases and pyrotechnics.

Even though the phone call had felt like a job interview at the time, she really hadn't expected anything to come from it. And she still didn't know how to respond.

She wanted to say yes, and she wanted to scream at them to lose her number.

It was just a reminder of that door she'd left open for him. A door that any sane person would've closed by now.

She took another drink of her favorite sweet red wine and set the glass down, then pressed the button.

Delete.

The doorbell rang, and she continued to sit. Dealing with people didn't sound like something she could do right now.

She got up and turned to her bedroom to get as far as she could from the door. After she got another glass of wine.

"Grace?" Her name shouted through the door reached her just as she was about to shut herself in her bedroom.

Her hand started to shake.

That was Liam's voice. Liam was at her door.

The bottle felt heavy and awkward as she headed for the door, gripping the bottle with both hands lest she drop it.

Opening locks and latches with her hands full of wine bottle didn't work. She bent and set the bottle on the floor. When she finally got the door open, the first thing she saw was his eyes.

Still dark blue. But hopeful. He'd shaved and the man's trademark stubble was gone, leaving that broad, manly jaw completely bare.

She looked down at his feet next. Wrapped, but not in the splint.

And wearing nice dark gray slacks and a button-down shirt. No tie, and also no sexy lean or smoldering looks. This wasn't Hollywood's Beautiful Bad Boy. This was...not a booty call.

This was him trying to make a good impression.

Without saying a word, she focused on the various things in his hands.

A bouquet of daisies and roses in the crook of one arm.

A heart-shaped box of candy in the crook of the other.

And in each hand a ceramic figurine. A kitten in one hand and a puppy in the other.

Her words came back to her.

Her old rewind fantasies.

Quintessential boyfriend gifts because…he had re-lationship feelings.

One hand flew to cover the base of her throat and she held back a cry that wanted to collapse her chest.

Worry in his eyes, Liam stayed standing there in front of her, waiting in silence.

It took her a minute, but when she managed a full breath without whimpering Grace lowered her hand again and folded her arms across her ribs. She wouldn't touch him. She wouldn't throw herself at him. He'd shown up, and that was a lot, but he had to say some stuff too.

Her stomach had just tied itself in a knot, and she probably couldn't even have moved from in front of the door if the apartment had been on fire.

Don't say the wrong thing.

She nodded to his hands. "What's all this?"

"It's candy, flowers, a kitten and a puppy," Liam said, not a hint of their usual flirtation in his tone. He looked nervous. And he sounded insane.

"The kitten and puppy were supposed to be real. And alive. Not ceramic."

"I'm new to commitment, Gracie. I didn't think I could handle taking on two animals if you told me to get lost so I went with figurines." He nodded to the apartment, and then to his arms. "Can I come in? Or can you take the breakables?"

"Are you here to ask me to go steady?" Even as she said the joking words, her heart leaped at the idea. It was a beginning. And they'd come this far. If he took this first step, he wouldn't turn back. Liam didn't know how to quit.

"Yes. And anything else you're willing to risk on me."

She unfolded her arms and opened the door wide enough to reach for the flowers and candy, relieving him of the items perched most precariously on his arms.

"Did I have four arms in your rewind fantasies? Or a pet carrier with the animals in it?"

"It's a lot to carry. I did say those fantasies were insane at the time." She stepped back from the door and nodded to him and the floor. "Don't kick the wine."

Turning to the hall table, she set down what she'd taken from him and then looked back, waiting. Afraid to let her hopes get too high. Terrified because they were already soaring.

"I had a long talk with your brother," Liam started. He stepped in and set the knickknacks down then closed the door.

"About me?"

Vulnerability, she saw it in his eyes. It was there in hers if he was looking closely enough, and he always looked closely. "And me."

His hands rubbed together roughly. He seemed to realize what he was doing and stuffed them into his pockets instead. "And also why he didn't tell me about your accident."

It was something she'd wondered too, but hadn't been able to bring herself to ask Nick yet. And right now it seemed very important for her to hear anything Liam wanted to bring up. Let him talk. At least as long as he had something to say he wouldn't go. She could hear his voice. Watch his mouth forming words—any words.

She could see that he'd nicked himself shaving before coming over.

"Why didn't he tell you? Was it because he knew about...my trench-coat antics?"

He shook his head.

"He didn't tell me when I called him, because it was the day my dad died." The words came softly, but he made no move to hide the rawness in his voice. "And he knew I'd still drop everything and run to your family at Cedars. He said it was the last thing I needed to deal with."

Grace nodded as she absorbed this. Nick had done what he'd thought was the kindest thing to do for Liam, and she might've made that same decision. He'd had no way of knowing what had been going on with them—she'd certainly never told anyone about the night she'd gone to his apartment. He'd probably only known they'd stopped talking about one another, if he was even perceptive enough to pick up on that at twenty. "That was probably the right thing to do."

"No, it wasn't," Liam said, taking a step closer to her, close enough to touch her if he wanted to. Or for her to touch him if she was brave enough. "It was an attempt at kindness, he did it because he cared. But the truth is... Cedars would've been the best place for me. I tried to make a family with my father when I got old enough, but we were both too damaged to know how. And when that ended, the best thing I could've done would've been to go to my real family. The best thing for me, I mean. You all had a lot to deal with at the time. So I could've understood if he'd not told me because you all couldn't deal with one more broken thing that day."

She still didn't know if she should touch him, but she needed to, and he needed it too. He'd come as close as he could and had left that final step to her, so close her head craned back and she could feel his breath fanning her skin. Accelerated, scared. She lifted a hand and rested her palm against the solid heat of his chest, and then used the other to brush away a trace of blood beside that razor nick. "That would never have happened."

"I know," he whispered, catching the hand at his jaw and holding it there while he looked down at her, his worry fading as fast as hers started to fall away.

"But I realized something after my talk with Nick. Something I'd been missing. Family takes care of each other, I got that part right. But the part I messed up is... real family never give up on one another. They never..." His eyes closed and he bowed his head forward until his forehead lightly touched hers. Slowly, his arms crept around her waist, the slightest tremble evident in his broad frame.

This was real. He was really doing this. It may not have come easily, but it did come. And she was going to say yes to whatever he offered because she'd learned those lessons early about how to treat the people you love, and he was still getting there.

"They never give up on someone they love," he said, as if touching strengthened him enough to go on. "My parents gave up. On life. On me. On everything. They worried about their desires first. When you were hurt, Nick didn't keep the information from me to keep me away from you or your family, he did it because he was trying to protect me. And maybe he was trying to protect you too, because you have terrible taste in men, Gracie."

She laughed, her hands moving up to cup his cheeks. "No, I don't. I had good taste when I picked you. But when it didn't work, all my efforts to find a stand-in

Liam failed. Turned out bad boys are easy to find but it was impossible to find one with your heart. With your charm. Your kindness and honor."

Tears rolled fat and wet from her eyes.

He tilted his head, kissed her eyes and nosed away the tears on her cheeks. "Don't cry. I don't ever want to make you cry again. If you'll still have me."

"What am I having you for?" She leaned back to look up at him once again, and slid her arms around his neck.

"Whatever you want. I'll take whatever I can get."

He held her gaze, those deep blue eyes open and full of love. He hadn't said it directly, but she'd known beyond doubt that he loved her since their only night together. She just hadn't believed she could wait for him to come around to the same knowledge.

"Do you want marriage?"

"I want you."

"Do you want children?"

He said again, "I want you."

"But you were worried about those things before, them being…contraindicated in a relationship with you."

"Contraindicated?"

"It's medical talk. It means don't mix this and that. Like ibuprofen and wine, and I suppose that in this case I'd be the ibuprofen…"

"You would certainly be the ibuprofen, you dull the pain and keep me upright. It's not sexy, but it's not wrong," he said, and then answered her question. "My objections have all been about the ways that I would screw it up and knowing I couldn't live with myself if I did. I told myself I didn't want marriage and children because I don't trust myself. I still don't trust that I'll have the right instincts. I've been terrified that I'd fail them and you. But after I talked to Nick, after I pieced together his motivation, my motivation, and your motivation, I realized what's been missing in me."

She shook her head, not understanding.

"When you Watsons screw up in relationships, when you make the wrong calls for the people you love? It's because you're trying to do what is best for them. When I've been making the wrong calls, it's been because I was afraid and trying to do what was best for me. But I know it now. I see the difference. I finally get it. And I know I can do better."

He stopped, tears standing in his vision. So open. If he said another word she'd break. They both needed a moment to touch before even one more word came. She tugged his head down, the barest urging needed.

His mouth closed on hers and he pressed her back, two steps and he had her once again against the entry wall. Only this time the need that drove him was toward closeness, to starved kisses, until they were both left gasping for air.

"Please take another chance on me." His forehead went back to hers, the rest of his body melding to hers. His words came slowly, with pauses for breath, but he didn't stop long enough to catch his breath properly. "I can promise, right now, that I'll want you. Forever. I'll love you forever."

He'd said it! Again a breathless laugh bubbled up, and she could only nod.

"Be patient when I screw up, because I'm going to screw up, I know I will, but I'll do it for the right reasons. Teach me how to make a life together—a real life, not some surface-deep Hollywood sham of a relationship. I want you, Gracie. I love you. And I understand now."

One tear fell onto her cheek, and then another. It took her a moment to realize they were his.

"One life, nothing held back. Deal?" Her voice, still not strong, wobbled over the words, and she smiled even as they both cried.

He nodded. "Deal."

"Now take me to bed."

He laughed, nodding and swooping her into his arms to head for the bedroom. And she let him. His ankle was wrapped, and it felt too good to be cradled against his chest.

She leaned up and kissed his ear, then nuzzled in close and whispered, "I got some new lacy black underwear...for next time..."

Because there would be a next time. A lifetime of next times.

* * * * *

MILLS & BOON®
Hardback – July 2016

ROMANCE

Di Sione's Innocent Conquest	Carol Marinelli
Capturing the Single Dad's Heart	Kate Hardy
The Billionaire's Ruthless Affair	Miranda Lee
A Virgin for Vasquez	Cathy Williams
Master of Her Innocence	Chantelle Shaw
Moretti's Marriage Command	Kate Hewitt
The Flaw in Raffaele's Revenge	Annie West
The Unwanted Conti Bride	Tara Pammi
Bought by Her Italian Boss	Dani Collins
Wedded for His Royal Duty	Susan Meier
His Cinderella Heiress	Marion Lennox
The Bridesmaid's Baby Bump	Kandy Shepherd
Bound by the Unborn Baby	Bella Bucannon
Taming Hollywood's Ultimate Playboy	Amalie Berlin
Winning Back His Doctor Bride	Tina Beckett
White Wedding for a Southern Belle	Susan Carlisle
Wedding Date with the Army Doc	Lynne Marshall
The Baby Inheritance	Maureen Child
Expecting the Rancher's Child	Sara Orwig
Doctor, Mummy...Wife?	Dianne Drake

MILLS & BOON®
Large Print – July 2016

ROMANCE

The Italian's Ruthless Seduction	Miranda Lee
Awakened by Her Desert Captor	Abby Green
A Forbidden Temptation	Anne Mather
A Vow to Secure His Legacy	Annie West
Carrying the King's Pride	Jennifer Hayward
Bound to the Tuscan Billionaire	Susan Stephens
Required to Wear the Tycoon's Ring	Maggie Cox
The Greek's Ready-Made Wife	Jennifer Faye
Crown Prince's Chosen Bride	Kandy Shepherd
Billionaire, Boss...Bridegroom?	Kate Hardy
Married for Their Miracle Baby	Soraya Lane

HISTORICAL

The Secrets of Wiscombe Chase	Christine Merrill
Rake Most Likely to Sin	Bronwyn Scott
An Earl in Want of a Wife	Laura Martin
The Highlander's Runaway Bride	Terri Brisbin
Lord Crayle's Secret World	Lara Temple

MEDICAL

A Daddy for Baby Zoe?	Fiona Lowe
A Love Against All Odds	Emily Forbes
Her Playboy's Proposal	Kate Hardy
One Night...with Her Boss	Annie O'Neil
A Mother for His Adopted Son	Lynne Marshall
A Kiss to Change Her Life	Karin Baine

MILLS & BOON®

Hardback – August 2016

ROMANCE

The Di Sione Secret Baby	Maya Blake
Carides's Forgotten Wife	Maisey Yates
The Playboy's Ruthless Pursuit	Miranda Lee
His Mistress for a Week	Melanie Milburne
Crowned for the Prince's Heir	Sharon Kendrick
In the Sheikh's Service	Susan Stephens
Marrying Her Royal Enemy	Jennifer Hayward
Claiming His Wedding Night	Louise Fuller
An Unlikely Bride for the Billionaire	Michelle Douglas
Falling for the Secret Millionaire	Kate Hardy
The Forbidden Prince	Alison Roberts
The Best Man's Guarded Heart	Katrina Cudmore
Seduced by the Sheikh Surgeon	Carol Marinelli
Challenging the Doctor Sheikh	Amalie Berlin
The Doctor She Always Dreamed Of	Wendy S. Marcus
The Nurse's Newborn Gift	Wendy S. Marcus
Tempting Nashville's Celebrity Doc	Amy Ruttan
Dr White's Baby Wish	Sue MacKay
For Baby's Sake	Janice Maynard
An Heir for the Billionaire	Kat Cantrell

MILLS & BOON®
Large Print – August 2016

ROMANCE

The Sicilian's Stolen Son — Lynne Graham
Seduced into Her Boss's Service — Cathy Williams
The Billionaire's Defiant Acquisition — Sharon Kendrick
One Night to Wedding Vows — Kim Lawrence
Engaged to Her Ravensdale Enemy — Melanie Milburne
A Diamond Deal with the Greek — Maya Blake
Inherited by Ferranti — Kate Hewitt
The Billionaire's Baby Swap — Rebecca Winters
The Wedding Planner's Big Day — Cara Colter
Holiday with the Best Man — Kate Hardy
Tempted by Her Tycoon Boss — Jennie Adams

HISTORICAL

The Widow and the Sheikh — Marguerite Kaye
Return of the Runaway — Sarah Mallory
Saved by Scandal's Heir — Janice Preston
Forbidden Nights with the Viscount — Julia Justiss
Bound by One Scandalous Night — Diane Gaston

MEDICAL

His Shock Valentine's Proposal — Amy Ruttan
Craving Her Ex-Army Doc — Amy Ruttan
The Man She Could Never Forget — Meredith Webber
The Nurse Who Stole His Heart — Alison Roberts
Her Holiday Miracle — Joanna Neil
Discovering Dr Riley — Annie Claydon

MILLS & BOON®

Why shop at millsandboon.co.uk?

Each year, thousands of romance readers find their perfect read at millsandboon.co.uk. That's because we're passionate about bringing you the very best romantic fiction. Here are some of the advantages of shopping at www.millsandboon.co.uk:

* **Get new books first**—you'll be able to buy your favourite books one month before they hit the shops

* **Get exclusive discounts**—you'll also be able to buy our specially created monthly collections, with up to 50% off the RRP

* **Find your favourite authors**—latest news, interviews and new releases for all your favourite authors and series on our website, plus ideas for what to try next

* **Join in**—once you've bought your favourite books, don't forget to register with us to rate, review and join in the discussions

Visit **www.millsandboon.co.uk**
for all this and more today!